HEMLOCK VALLEY

VOLUME ONE

SUNNY A MORGAN

SKYLAR QUINN

HEMLOCK VALLEY VOLUME ONE

First edition. May 2025

Published May 23, 2025

Cover Photo: AdobeStock_182152598; Deposit Photo Image: 139904126 Owner: studiostoks

Other images used inside of this book are from: Deposit Photo Image: 140283350 Owner: vectorpocket; Deposit Photo Image: 59095517 Copyright @ mast3r; Deposit Photo Image: 140283350 Owner: vectorpocket; Deposit Photo Image: 177408598 Copyright @ Maxutov; Deposit Photo Image: 691142114 Owner: AdamLevy; Deposit Photo Image: 144685677 Copyright @ Yafimava; Deposit Photo Image: 213566402 Owner: toricheks2016.gmail.com; Deposit Photo Image: 135082866 Copyright @ smeagorl; Deposit Photo Image: 741675558 Copyright @ juliarstudio; Deposit Photo Image: 225943786 Copyright @ comicstocks@ gmail.com

Edited by Leslie Bardal (Caught By A Vampire, Sneaking Around With A Tiger, Leprechaun Caught My tongue)

Written by Sunny A Morgan & Skylar Quinn

ISBN# 978-1-941194-29-4

CRUSH Publications

www.crushpublications.com

CONTENTS

SNEAKING AROUND WITH A TIGER
Skylar Quinn

WEREWOLF TAKES A MATE
Sunny A Morgan

LEPRECHAUN CAUGHT MY TONGUE
Skylar Quinn

CHASING GHOSTS
Sunny A Morgan

EASTER BUNNY MADE ME DO IT
Skylar Quinn

WELCOME TO HEMLOCK VALLEY

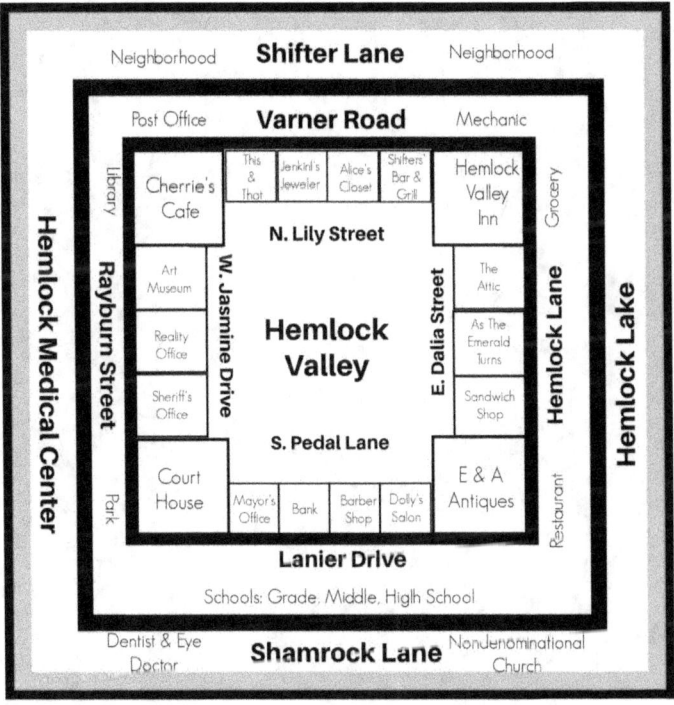

HEMLOCK VALLEY

LOOK WHAT THE CAT DRAGGED IN

SUNNY A MORGAN

PREFACE

FOUR YEARS AGO

JEMMA

I heard Leo running after me. "Jemma, goddamn it! Get your ass back here!"

I kept running, refusing to stop until my knees buckled, and I fell to the soggy ground. The warm wind whipped around me. Lightning flashed in the distance, lighting up the black sky. I lifted my face to the wind and the night, letting it beat mercilessly around my body.

Tears pooled in my eyes, burning from the wind and debris. My grandmother always told me love wasn't a fairy-tale. It wasn't for the faint of heart. True love was dark and light, kind, and cruel. This was all dark, all cruel.

"Let me go." I cried when he fell down beside me.

"No." He growled.

Leo carried me to his house, and we made love. I snuck out in the wee hours of the morning. Leaving him and Hemlock Valley.

Why did I let myself love him? Love never lasts.

CHAPTER 1

LEO

I left four years ago. I swore I'd never return, but my family needed me. My father died, and it didn't matter if I was returning to the place that broke my heart.

I looked around the bar. Soft lights filtered through the exposed wooden beams. This was home. This was my family's legacy. In historic downtown Hemlock sits this old bar. Shifters' had been our family's legacy since it opened its doors in nineteen sixty-two.

I felt our family's history and the secrets these walls held, and I couldn't help but smile. Tradition. Home.

"Welcome to Shifters, I'm Jolie." A cute blonde server greeted a table to my right. She cocked her hip, tilting her head to study the college boys. "What can I get you guys?" She asked.

"I think I'll have Jolie straight up." One kid grinned.

"Sorry, we had to take her off the menu. She's been known to be deadly." Jolie smirked and turned toward the rest of the table. "What can I get you three?"

"Your best whiskey doubles all around, sweetheart." The biggest of the four guys said.

"Celebrating?" she asked.

"Something like that," One of them answered.

"Best whiskey all around, right?" Jolie smiled, asking all of them.

"Unless Jolie straight up became available recently?" The first guy smirked.

"Sorry, she still is too deadly to be on the menu." She winked and sashayed off.

"She's mine." Asher announced.

CHAPTER 2

LEO

I felt her before I saw her, before I heard her. The air prickled with life, thunder in my ears, and when my eyes followed the voice behind me. I froze.

"Leo?" her soft voice whispered.

I didn't want to turn, but I had to. I had to see her face again. "Jemma."

"I didn't know you were back." She said, shifting nervously.

"Of course, I'm back. No one could keep me from my family during this time." My patience snapped.

"I didn't mean–" She started before thrusting a casserole dish in my arms. "I need to go," Jemma said, her voice cracking as she ran out the door.

Her voice poured out of her soul and allowed you a glimpse into the woman behind the curtain of auburn hair. She used to shield her from the world. Before I knew what I was doing, my lion was dragging me across the bar in a flash. Following her down the street.

"Jemma?" I called behind her. She looked over her shoulder. I saw the flint of curiosity and fear in her eyes. I also saw a bruise on her cheek when the light hit her face. Man and lion growled.

She took a few more steps before she stopped and turned down an alley. "What do you want from me?" She asked, her hand went to her chest.

"Why are you back?" I asked.

"A few days ago, I returned. I heard about your dad and wanted to pay my respects to your family. Why are you back?" She asked.

"I'm back for my family." I whispered in her ear. "And for good."

"I have to go." She rushed out the words, stepping away from me.

"Wait." I grasped her wrist, giving it a slight pull toward me.

She looked down at my hand wrapped around her wrist, then into my eyes. Fear. Then, I noticed her cheek again, swollen, a with small cut.

"What happened, little witch?" I lifted my free hand, brushing her swollen cheek lightly. Anger filled my gut. Who did this to her?

Tears glistened in her eyes. She shook her head. "I have to go." She turned and ran down the alley, leaving me watching her with a need to follow her and claim her burning in my veins.

Fuck, I haven't felt my lion this excited and pissed off in years. Since she left us four years ago. The animal clawed at my insides for me to follow her, to hunt her down. To claim her.

I was greeted by my older brother, Asher, when I walked back into the bar. "Take it easy on her."

"What?" I hissed.

"Calm down, little brother. She's had a rough four years." Asher said.

"She isn't the only one." I growled. "Why is she even in Hemlock? She left four years ago."

"I don't know, but she returned a few days ago with bruises and one suitcase." Asher said with a shake of his head.

"She had a bruise. Does she have an abusive boyfriend, husband?" I asked.

"Who knows, but try to leave your past pain behind when talking to Jemma." Asher clapped my shoulder before walking back behind the bar.

CHAPTER 3

JEMMA

*W*hy did I come back here? Seeing Leo forced all the emotions I had been shoving away come forward. I never expected to feel his lion again. But I felt it trying to connect with me.

"Jemma? Earth to Jemma." Ariel, my best friend, interrupted my thoughts, snapping her fingers. "Are you in there?"

"Sorry." I said, shaking my head. "What's up?"

Ariel chuckled. "You aren't even dressed yet."

"I don't think I should go." I said.

"Jemma, you have to go. I need a wing woman."

"You don't need me, Ariel." I sighed.

Ariel took my hand. "You deserve to have some fun. Stop thinking about Leo and the hell you left in California."

"Easier said than done." I protested.

She rolled her eyes. "Come on."

"Fine, I'll go." I huffed and walked into my closet to find an outfit.

"Nothing frumpy." Ariel said, shoving a red dress in my

hands. "You're never going to get laid looking sad and pathetic."

"I don't need to get laid." I quipped back.

"The fuck you don't, and if you're not going to fuck Leo, you need to fuck someone." Ariel laughed.

An hour later, we were walking into Attic. Music was playing, people were dancing, and laughter filled the bar.

"Let's dance." Ariel grabbed my hand, dragging me to the dance floor. We are only on the floor a few minutes before two guys make their move.

The blonde leaned into me. "I'm Derek. What's your name, beautiful?" He asked, his hot breath against my earlobe.

"Jemma," I answer, tilting my head to look at him better. He is hot, but he doesn't give me goosebumps or make my pussy ache with the need to have his cock inside me. Only Leo does that to my body.

"Do you mind?" Derek asked.

For a second, I was confused, and then I realized he had asked if he could dance with me. I smiled and nodded my head. I made the best of it and forgot about Leo. Derek's hand lands on my waist firmly. He guided our movements, and I let myself go, moving to the rhythm of the music.

"You don't remember me, do you?" Derek yelled over the music.

"Sorry, no I don't." I called back.

"I'm Leo's cousin. We only met a couple of times." He said.

I nodded, trying to think back to Leo's family I had met in the past. But I couldn't place him.

By the third song, I've let the music melt away all thoughts of Leo. Derek became more aggressive. His hands wandered to my ass, squeezing my cheeks painfully. He pressed himself into my body, pushing his leg between my thighs. I tried to pull away, but his hands wouldn't allow me to move.

"Let me go," I demand, my hands pushing his chest. I can feel his erection against my thigh, and I want to vomit. "Get your fucking hands off of me, or I will scream," I growled.

The fucker laughed. "You are still a fucking tease. And scream, no one will hear you or care." One of his hands grabbed my breast, pawing it in his meaty hand. "Girls who dress like little sluts are begging for it." His handsome face turned into a lecherous leer.

"Get your fucking hands off of her, now." A male voice demanded from behind me. I knew that deep, masculine voice anywhere. Leo. I felt Derek's hands being forcefully removed from my body. I looked up at Leo as he shoved Derek completely away from me.

"What the fuck, man?" Derek sneered.

"Dance is over, and if you want to walk out of here, you better get moving now." Leo was a big guy, muscle packed on top of muscle, and he was six foot four. "Go home and sleep it off."

Leo took me in his arms and started to dance with me. "Thank you. What are you doing here?" I asked.

"I could ask you the same thing." He countered, taking me in his arms, and started dancing with me.

"Girls' Night out." I offered.

"Guys' Night out." He shrugged. "It was a good thing because it looked like you needed help."

I glared at him. "I could have handled it."

His face turned hard. "It never should have happened." He hissed in my ear. "Another man touched you and thought he could get into your tight little pussy."

One of his hands slid to my hip and moved down to my thigh. "Were you going to let him inside your little pussy? Let another man touch what's mine?" His fingers dug into my thigh.

Anger pulsed through me, and I tried to pull away. "I'm not yours."

He swatted my ass. "You are mine."

"You don't even like me." I said.

"Whether I like you has nothing to do with whether you are mine." Leo hissed.

I could feel his lion pulsing, ready to come out. Fucking hell, Leo was turned on. He was pissed, but he was fucking ready to pounce. If I was honest, I was ready to let him.

"I should have never let you leave. I should have tied you to my bed. Fuck, I should have come after you."

"Why didn't you?" I asked. Not sure I wanted the answer.

His eyes softened, and the back of his hand caressed my cheek. "Ego, pride, embarrassment."

"I had no choice." I whispered.

He shook his head. "Not tonight. Tonight, be mine."

"This is a bad idea." I said.

"Fuck, it's a terrible idea, but I don't give a fuck. I need to feel you. My lion needs to feel you."

CHAPTER 4

"$\mathcal{I}$ don't think we should, Leo," I whispered yelled.

"Why not?" Leo asked, slipping his hand under my dress.

"Because we're in a bar bathroom," I reminded him. "We aren't kids anymore."

"We aren't dead either." He replied against my lips. "I can't wait to be inside you a minute longer."

He gave me a deep kiss and then lifted my dress and turned me towards the mirror. With his hand in the middle of my back, he pushed me to lean over the vanity and commanded. "Lean over."

I was relieved that at least the bathroom was clean. Glancing at my reflection in the mirror, I felt his erection press against my lace-covered backside. I looked desperate, flushed, and on the verge of spilling out of my dress. As I met his gaze in the mirror, my eyes dilated. He wore his trademark smirk on his lips.

"Anyone could hear us or walk in." I said.

He pressed his body against mine, his breath hot on my neck. "That's what makes it so exciting, Jemma," he whispered.

His hand slipped under my lace underwear and pushed it aside, revealing my wet and swollen pussy. "You're already so wet," he murmured. He removed my panties from my feet and positioned himself behind me.

"I can't believe we're doing this," I said.

Leo couldn't resist the urge any longer and thrust himself deep inside me, causing my body to tremble with pleasure. All my protests left the moment his cock was inside of me. "Watch us. I want to see your pretty eyes as I fuck you. I want to see all the shades of blue they turn the closer you get to release."

I looked up and saw his amber eyes, which burned with fire. My body responded to him as it always did. Four years later and I still responded like a wanton woman with him.

He forcefully pulled down the front of my dress and grabbed my tits, pinching my nipples hard. This caused my pussy to spasm. He felt incredible inside of me. He pulled his hips back, and his cock almost slipped out of me before he lunged forward again. I cried out and held onto the edges of the vanity.

"You feel so good," he growled, the sound animalistic. "How do I feel inside of you?"

I could not respond; I simply stared at his face and tightened my muscles around him, squeezing his cock. Despite the pain in my hips from being pounded into the sink, I didn't care. I just wanted him to keep fucking me. I didn't give a damn if the entire bar was waiting outside the bathroom door. "Yes, fuck yes," I chanted.

His face twisted in pleasure, and his cock swelled. He was close, and so was I. "Harder," I cried.

He pounded into me, savagely ravaging my pussy. "Whose pussy is this? Who does it belong to?" he demanded, slamming into me over and over again. "Jemma," he warned, slowing his movements.

He had always enjoyed teasing me and not allowing me to

cum until he got his answers. Sometimes, I ignored him, and he would eventually give in and let me cum. But tonight, I would cave. It's been too long without him.

"I belong to you. You own my body and my pussy," I said, my voice on the brink of tears, desperate to climax.

"That's right, Jemma" he purred. He continued to thrust a few more times, and I exploded in ecstasy. "And your heart?"

"Always you." It was true, but I shouldn't have said it.

"It's always been us, Jemma." We both collapsed against the sink, panting heavily. As we caught our breath, we gazed at each other in the mirror. He smiled and winked at me before saying, "Let's get you cleaned up, little witch."

After a few minutes, we left the bathroom. Even though I felt like everyone knew what we were doing, no one said anything.

CHAPTER 5

LEO

"*L*et's go." My voice was rough and thick with lust, and my lips brushed against the shell of her ear. I told Jemma to let Ariel know she was leaving, and my brother would take her home.

"Out of the dress," I growled.

I noted the change in Jemma's breathing when she obeyed my command. She enjoyed taking orders. "Such a good little witch." I praised, and she rewarded me with a smile. "Come here." I beckoned with a crook of my finger.

Again, she obeyed immediately. My enormous arms wrapped around her body, drawing her into my frame. I held her for several seconds, breathing her in, letting my hand slowly stroke along her back, causing her to shiver. She tilted her head up to look at me. Her eyes searched for something. Maybe a sign that this was real, and I wouldn't push her away.

I know I was searching her eyes for hope that this was real. She was mine.

Her gaze landed and locked on my mouth. I saw the hunger that blazed in her eyes. She wanted to kiss me. Heat strummed through my body as she continued to stare at my mouth. Her pink tongue slipped between her full lips. She slowly licked her bottom lip. Kissing Jemma was like nothing I had experienced before. I enjoyed kissing women, but with Jemma, it was more. More powerful, more heated, more desperate, more everything. She lifted her gaze from my mouth, scanning my face. Her dainty fingers touched my jawline and slid slowly down my throat. Everything inside me screamed to fuck her. To stop this torture. But I needed to give her this after I was such a brute to her at the Attic. Give her time to explore. My pulse thrummed under her touch.

"Is this real?" She asked in a small, sweet voice.

"It's real. You're mine. There's no going back." My voice filled with raw lust. She stepped up on her toes and pressed her mouth to my throat. I felt her inhale deeply, breathing me into her. It felt primal. My witch was a lioness, not a kitten. She licked along my throat, and I moaned as she lapped at my pulse. I couldn't take it any longer. I pulled back, grasping her biceps. I searched her eyes and saw the need and hunger. I knew it was the same hunger and need my eyes held.

"Be sure this is what you want." I snarled the words. I needed to know she was sure because I wouldn't let her go after being inside her again.

"I want you, Leo; it's always been you." Her blue eyes almost looked black with her desire.

"Damn it, run from me, but thank fuck you aren't." I snarled.

Jemma kissed the corner of my mouth again before shifting her lips to my mouth. Nibbling lightly between kisses, urging me to open for her. I did not stop her from kissing me, but I didn't return her kiss. I enjoyed her coaxing me to open, enjoyed her becoming bolder.

"Don't you want to kiss me?" She finally asked. I stared at her for half a second before my mouth covered hers. My nostrils flared, my hands plunged into her hair, and my fingers dug into her scalp. My tongue warred with hers. My mouth and tongue became aggressive. I kept one hand in her hair and guided our kiss. My other hand went to her waist, and my arm locked her to my body as I walked her backward until she hit the edge of the bed. I removed my lips from hers, long enough to demand.

"Center of the bed, arms above your head, knees up, feet on the mattress flat, and legs spread wide." I barely recognized my graveled voice.

CHAPTER 6

JEMMA

*M*y heart slammed against my chest in a rhythmic beat that guided my desire. I followed Leo's orders and positioned myself on the bed. My eyes never left his hungry gaze. My body was on fire from my head to my toes. The unbearable anticipation and the overwhelming need to have him claim me once and for all had me close to exploding. He hadn't even entered me yet. He just stared at me like a predator. Leo's hands pushed my knees further apart, spreading me open for his view. Liquid heat pooled in my pussy and trickled down my thighs. I knew he saw my juices, but I felt no shame. I was beyond any stage of embarrassment. I wanted him too badly. I needed him to see how much I loved everything he did to me. How much I craved him. How sorry I was for everything.

He licked his lips and slowly kneeled before me. "So pretty and wet." He purred, maneuvering his shoulders between my legs. "Mmm, now this is what I have been waiting for, Jemma," he whispered. "All this cream just for me. It's just begging me to lap it up."

The muscles inside my pussy clenched. Leo dropped his head and nuzzled his cheek against my thigh. Then he placed a string of wet kisses along my thigh and trailed over my hipbone. His teeth lightly scraped at my tender flesh. My breath came out in tiny pants. So many sensations, Leo between my legs. His fingers dug into my skin as his tongue finally made its tortuous trip to my wet folds. He flicked his tongue along my slit. I needed more. I needed him to speed up.

"Please," I begged.

"I love hearing you beg," Leo whispered, easing my pussy lips apart, revealing my swollen clit. His tongue lightly teased the bud. "Your cunt cries out to me, begs for me. Do you know what that does to a man? Does to me? To my lion? To see how much you need me to fuck you. To claim you."

I wanted to push up on my elbows to watch him, but I didn't think I could do so without passing out. My mind and body spun out of control with my desire.

"Please," I moaned, lifting my hips and begging for more.

"Soon but first." He said nothing else, but drove his tongue inside my pussy. I cried out again. My hips lifted instinctually, and my fingers gripped the blanket as my body uncontrollably writhed under his assault. At that moment, I believed anything was possible and that I could not live without this, without him. Slowly, his tongue eased from my body.

Leo lifted his head, and he looked into my eyes. "Fucking delicious. Nothing tastes better than your pussy juices."

I gaped at him, my body on fire. I needed more. "Don't stop," I whimpered.

"Oh, we've just started. Tonight's dinner is one I plan to savor." He laughed wickedly. His eyes were now completely black. Once again, he dropped his head, and his deliciously wicked tongue made a long lap over my entire pussy. Sounds I didn't recognize poured from my mouth. My thighs trembled, and gooseflesh appeared on every inch of my body as he continued to circle his tongue slowly around my sensitive bud.

When his lips finally closed around my clit and he suckled, I came with a scream. "Leo!" My body writhed under him and my head thrashed from side to side. A growl escaped his throat, and his tongue continued to work my body. He forced my legs further apart so he could bury his face between my thighs. His tongue never eased its onslaught. I felt tears stream down my cheeks. I tried to stop them from falling, but everything became too much. Every dream I ever had of a life with him flooded my senses. I felt open and raw. It was all too much. His tongue fucked me fast and hard, and his growls intensified until I came again. My pussy pressed against his unshaven chin as my body continued to convulse from wave after wave of my orgasm pulsing through my body. Leo shifted my boneless body and settled me further into the bed.

"I need to fuck you," he growled, looming over me.

"Wait," my breathless voice commanded.

"What?" His tone was impatient and bordered on violence. "It's too late to change your mind. If I'm not inside you soon, I will not survive."

"I need to tell you." I asked. I hated how pathetic I sounded.

"What?"

I lifted my eyes, tears still burning. "Never mind."

CHAPTER 7

LEO

*M*y nostrils flared. I did not want to talk. I needed to be inside Jemma, fucking her into another world. I made myself clear before we started this, but the confused look in her eyes mingled with her lust had me pushing for answers.

"Tell me."

"I didn't want to leave you. I had to protect you from my grandmother. She hated shifters and–" Jemma sighed.

"Baby, we can talk about all this later, but right now, I need to fuck you. Are you good with that?" I demanded.

She nodded and gave me a small smile. "Then what are you waiting for?"

"No more talking, little witch. We can use our mouths for so many other things." I leaned down and kissed her lips before I dropped my head lower and took one pebbled nipple into my mouth.

"Yes," she breathed, arching up into my body. My tongue circled her nipple, flickering back and forth over the rose-colored bud. She moaned beneath me. I groaned at the feel of her small hand wrapping around my cock.

Her thumb swiped over the pre-cum, and she gripped me tighter and my hand slid down her body. My hand trailed over her ribcage, down her hips, splaying flat across her stomach until I found her sex. She was on fire, her cream was molten lava, and I nearly came. My teeth grazed over her nipple.

"Ah, baby, your body is so hot and wet."

"Leo." She moaned, and her hand slid up and down my length. Growling, I shoved two fingers inside her pussy. Her body sucked my fingers in, squeezing so tight that I had to bite down the urge to release my seed in her hand. I watched her eyes widen with each thrust into her body, her perfect mouth slightly parted, and the rise and fall of her chest became too much.

"Fuck, Jemma. I need inside you." I growled as I took her mouth possessively. My fingers plunged deep inside.

"Please, I need you cock fucking me," she begged between brutal kisses. That was all I needed to hear. My fingers eased from Jemma's body, and my cock replaced them instantly. I looked down at her pink folds, hugging my cockhead before pushing myself in deep.

Slowly, I pulled from her scolding heat, savoring the feel of her body encompassing me completely when I thrust back inside. My hands slid under her hips, and I grasped her perfect ass. I lifted her body to take more of me. I have felt nothing like being inside her. I thought it was amazing fucking her violently at the bar, but this was perfection. I pushed her into the mattress, spreading her legs.

My hands-on her thighs, and I thrust. "Yes," she hissed.

"You're so tight. I'm not sure how long I can last." I said through gritted teeth. The need to go faster barreled through me. Her head thrashed from side to side, body writhing on the mattress. I slowly pulled out. I had to see our connection again. To remind me, this was real. Jemma's swollen pink pussy lips wrapped around my cock, coating me in her juices. It was a beautiful sight. I dipped my head and took one luscious nipple into my mouth, drawing on it hard.

God, I wanted to fuck and eat her at the same time. Pumping in and out of her as she strangled my dick, her body sent electrical shock waves around me. She was close. I could feel it, thank God, because I was about to explode.

"Leo!" she screamed as she started to cum. I speed up my movement, going deeper and harder. I battered into Jemma's cunt, hitting her cervix as she came around me.

An animalistic rage filled my body, and I rammed ruthlessly into her tight pussy. I cursed in pleasure each time another wave of her orgasm clamped down on my cock. I needed to stamp my claim on her and fill her cunt with my seed. I roared as my cum shot out of me like a geyser, spraying her insides, claiming her, and hopefully breeding my little witch. I stayed buried deep inside her even after the last of my release was gone. I lowered my forehead to hers. I claimed her tempting mouth in a leisurely kiss. Even with my slow exploration of her mouth, the kiss was possessive. It was a promise. A claiming.

"I love you," I whispered against her lips.

She smiled and nipped my bottom lip. "I love you too, Leo."

CHAPTER 8

LEO

*a*n empty bed greeted me when I woke up. I hissed in anger, and my lion wanted to spring free to chase down its mate.

I pulled on jeans and a t-shirt when I noticed a note on the side table.

I'm not running. I'm meeting my mother. I didn't want to wake you.
Text me
555-777-1414
~Jem

I picked up my phone and sent a text before adding her as a contact.

Me: Meet me at Cherrie's for lunch

Jemma: Okay

JEMMA

"Jemma, take a seat anywhere." Cherrie called as I walked in.

I decided a booth in the back was the best choice. The bell rang over the door and Leo walked in. I could feel my cheeks flush under his intense gaze as he walked to the table.

"Jemma." His voice sent shivers down my spine.

"Hi."

Once he sat beside me, I started. "Leo, let me talk. I need to explain what happened four years ago." I took a deep breath. "I never knew who my father was until four years ago. He needed my help, my power. I refused at first, but he threatened you and my mother. I didn't believe he could do anything, but he did. Benjamin Debois killed my grandmother. My grandmother was the most powerful witch in our coven, and he could kill her. Maybe if I wasn't devastated over her death, I could have thought of a way to fix things. But I believed he would kill you and my mother, too. So, I left with him."

"Where is he now?" Leo asked.

"I killed him." I looked away as I continued. "He spent so much time training me and developing my powers, he didn't realize I was getting stronger than him. I never wanted to leave you and I didn't want to tell you because I knew you would stop me. I'm so sorry."

Leo grabbed my chin and forced me to look at him. "Why did he need you?"

"Revenge, power, money. He was never clear except that my grandmother destroyed his tribe. Killed his father. Since I've been back, I asked my mother about him. She said his tribe was dangerous and evil. She always felt guilty for bringing him into the family. My father seduced her, and she believed he was special. She loved him, but when she became pregnant with me, he left until he returned four years ago." I touched Leo's cheek. "That's all I know right now. I know I need more information to protect my family, and I will get it. Hopefully, with your help?"

He leaned in and kissed me. "I've got you." He said against my lips.

"Thank you." I said. "Now let's eat. I have missed Cherrie's pot roast."

Leo shook his head and laughed. "Gods I missed you."

CHAPTER 9

JEMMA

"*W*hy did you want to come to Attic instead of Shifters tonight?" I asked.

"I have plans that I can not do at my family's bar." He smirked.

"What plans?" I asked.

"Jemma," His voice full of warning. He did not want to play.

I could feel his warm breath on my cheek as he leaned in close to be heard over the music. He moved in and kissed me. The kiss was chaste, but it still affected my body. "Open your legs," Leo demanded against my lips.

He leaned back in his chair, took a swig from his beer bottle, his eyes never leaving mine. I knew what was next, and I couldn't believe he was going to do this.

"Are you serious?" I asked.

He had a wicked way of getting me to do things I normally would never consider. Leo sipped his beer with an arched brow, patiently waiting for me to comply. We both knew I would do as he asked.

"Jemma, spread those sexy legs of yours." He demanded.

"I'm not sure how I let you talk me into such things." I said, shaking my head. I scooted closer to him and spread my legs. His hand slipped under my fifties style full circle skirt. I giggled when he grumbled about his hand getting lost in the toile skirting under my dress.

"My struggle is funny, sweetheart?" He cocked his head and looked into my eyes. I took a sip of my beer and almost spit it out when I felt his finger slide under my panties. He smirked as I closed my legs around his hand. "Jemma." His eyes darkened with a mischievous glint to them.

I opened my thighs, allowing him access to my center. We spent the next thirty minutes chatting as if he was not fingering my pussy in a bar. Finally, Leo paid the bill and grabbed my hand. He led me quickly outside.

We walked to his motorcycle. I gasped when he pushed me over onto the seat. He haphazardly tossed my dress up over my hips. "What are you doing?" I whispered.

He didn't answer, but lowered himself to his knees, pulled my panties to the side, and his tongue lapped along my pussy. He flicked his tongue against my clit, and I couldn't stop the moan that he pulled from me.

"What if someone sees us?" I asked, my eyes darting around the parking lot. "I don't —" I started, but his fingers spread my swollen, wet lips apart and he sucked my clit into his mouth.

"Leo," his name melted into a soft moan as his tongue swirled between my swollen lips and two thick fingers thrust inside my pussy. I became wetter, my arousal quickly growing as he continued to fuck my pussy with his fingers and circle my clit with his tongue. I whimpered and my fingers gripped the leather bike seat. His lips went back to my clit and sucked as his finger fucked me into oblivion.

My moans and cries echoed in the night air, and I no longer cared about someone seeing us. "Leo, fuck. So good," my thighs shook, and my orgasm tore through me like an electrical wave. I bucked against his mouth, wildly thrashing and moaning.

Leo stood, and I whimpered at the loss of his mouth until he slammed his cock into my pussy in one hard thrust. He slammed into me over and over again with feverish urgency.

"Fuck Sweetheart," he growled before his mouth sucked the pulse in my neck.

He controlled my body, and I happily let him. His mouth traveled down the column of my neck. "I'm going to cum, Leo," I cried.

"Not yet," he growled. Slamming frantically into my body. "I'm going to fill you with my cum. I want it dripping down your legs, but not until you beg for it," he hissed with a thrust of his hips.

"Leo!" I cried out.

"Beg, little witch," he grated as he plunged in and out of my sex. I squeezed my vaginal walls around his cock.

"I'm close," I cried out again.

He slowed his movements, and I groaned in frustration. "Beg."

I tightened my pussy around his length, sucking his cock deeper inside my heat. He growled, "beg, Jemma."

"You beg," I hissed.

He chuckled and pulled himself from my body. He turned me around and helped me sit on his bike. "Always stubborn," he said, shaking his head as he tucked himself back into his jeans. "We'll fix that when we get home."

I bit my bottom lip and tried to stop the grin from forming on my face. I couldn't wait.

HEMLOCK VALLEY

CAUGHT BY
A VAMPIRE

SKYLAR QUINN

CHAPTER 1

LOCATION: AS THE EMERALD TURNS — RAVEN

*H*emlock Valley had been home to creatures of the night for so many years that when something mysterious happened in the city, the state police never questioned the local authorities. They rarely showed up in our town. Sheriff Robert Jackson and his Deputy Jason Walker handled every case, day or night, and no one ever questioned their findings. So, when the state police pulled up to my bookstore "As the Emerald Turns," I knew the news would be bad.

"Willa, something's going on, state police are outside."

"I know, I called them." Willa looked at me with the darkest stare I had ever seen coming from my best friend.

"Why didn't you call Sheriff Jackson?"

She shook her head. "This goes far beyond him."

Ice ran through my blood as I watched her stand up from her reading chair and walk towards the door. As the officer pushed the glass barrier open, my heart sank, waiting in anticipation of what was about to transpire.

"Ladies, I'm looking for Willa Sims."

"I'm the one who called you," she said, extending her hand out in normal societal pleasantries.

"Ma'am, I'm officer Timothy Jacobs. Can we go somewhere to talk?" He walked deeper into our bookstore and started looking around. I couldn't help the feeling that he was judging us somehow.

"This is my business partner Raven Burk,e she's going to want to know what I have to say too. She can listen." Willa showed the officer to the back of our bookstore and offered him a seat at our book signing table.

"It's unusual for us to get a call about something going on in this town. Have you spoken to your sheriff?"

Willa shook her head no, "This doesn't concern him. This concerns you, specifically you."

I watched in silence as he pulled out his notebook and started taking notes. "What do you mean, me?"

She didn't miss a beat. She reached over to her basket and pulled out her deck of cards. Her Tarot cards. She shuffled them as she watched him with a strict intent to get a sense from him.

"Ma'am, can you put the cards down?"

"Only after you cut them," she said. Willa placed the cards in front of the officer, and I watched as they had a staring contest.

"Ma'am, I have serious work to do."

She nodded, "As do I officer, please cut."

Officer Jacobs looked at me. All I could do was shrug my shoulders and smile. "She won't let it go."

"Fine, here." He reached out, cut the deck of cards, and went back to his notebook. "Please, what is this about?"

I watched as Willa started laying out the cards in the form of a reading. I almost missed the words she was saying as I looked down at what cards had now been put on display.

"Do you know anything about our town, officer?"

He nodded his head. "I know enough to stay away unless I am called in. Like I was today."

Willa looked down at the cards and then up at the officer. After doing this a couple of times, she opened her mouth. Before she spoke, I could feel the temperature of the room change. The chill ran over my skin, goosebumps popping up along my arms.

"Do you believe in the afterlife, Officer Jacobs?"

"I believe in God, heaven, and hell. If that's what you mean."

She shook her head. "I mean, do you believe that when we die, spirits are left behind with unfinished business?"

"No, ma'am. I don't believe in that. What does that have to do with why you called me here?"

Willa looked over at me and then looked back at Officer Jacobs. "Your mother's killer is still around in this city, and she wants you to solve the case."

"Excuse me," he said, "is this some game to you? A joke?"

"No, sir, your mother is talking to me. Right now, in fact." Willa pointed to the tarot card on the table and said, "Right here, see, this one shows you have unfinished business."

"I knew coming here today was a mistake. This is preposterous. The world doesn't have spirits that talk in real life." Officer Jacobs pushed himself away from the table and stood up with a rage that made me shiver.

"Wait, please," Willa begged.

"No, and I would appreciate it if you didn't call me again." He walked towards the front door and as he was about to leave, the room's temperature chilled even further.

"She's here right now, Mable, your mom. She said for me to tell you that Autumn is still alive, and she is right here in this town."

I watched him turn around, as if he had seen a ghost.

"Autumn? How do you know about her?" His voice came

out with an aggression that told me something horrible had happened in his past.

"Your mom. She wants you to know I'm telling the truth. She wants you to find her killer."

"You two are nut jobs and if you ever contact me again, I will arrest you for harassment!" Officer Jacobs turned around and stormed out of the bookstore. The glass door slammed behind him as he vanished into his police car.

"Well," I said with a shock, "That wasn't on my bingo card for today. You didn't think a heads up would be good," I chuckled.

Willa smiled, "I know how much you love when my powers freak people out."

"Yeah, I do. But this guy seemed way more than freaked out. Especially when you mentioned Autumn. By the way, who the hell is that?"

"The PTA president at the high school."

I gave Willa the "You gotta be kidding me" look. "No, we're not getting involved with the PTA. They drive us nuts."

She laughed, "No, we aren't. Officer Jacobs is."

"Yeah, I don't think he is going to come back here again. He looked freaked out and was not happy with you at all."

"For now, but before the end of the week, he'll be back. His mom is confident of it."

"Do you know who killed his mother?"

Willa smirked, "Now, where is the fun in that?"

I sighed. It was always a good mystery with her.

CHAPTER 2

LOCATION: HEMLOCK VALLEY HIGH SCHOOL —
TIMOTHY

I knew that taking the call into Hemlock Valley would be one that I regretted. Why I went against my gut was beyond me, but here I was, driving away from this book shop with a knot in the pit of my stomach that would probably give me indigestion for a week. Willa Sims had made my blood turn ice cold, mentioning my mother's murder.

My beautiful mother. Taken from my family way too early. She would have been celebrating her sixtieth birthday this year. I'll never forget when the officer showed up at our house to tell us what had happened. My Aunt Suzie was with me. She had come over to help take care of my younger sister and I. My mother was working late at the hospital. Aunt Suzie wasn't really our aunt, but she was like family to us. After all, she was my sister's godmother, so that made her family.

Aunt Suzie had made us homemade lasagna. Her grandmother taught her how to cook it when she went over to Italy one summer. My sister Vicky loved it and learned how to duplicate it. But I can't ever take a bite of lasagna again. Just thinking about it makes my stomach churn.

The officer knocked on our door and when Aunt Suzie opened it, I knew bad news was waiting for us. I saw her tears before I registered the words he had said.

"I regret to inform you that Mabel Jacobs was found tonight behind a dumpster. She was leaving her shift at the hospital, from what we can tell."

Those were the only words I remember. I was in eighth grade, Vicky was in fourth. Nothing about that night sits well with me, even now as I look back. It was part of the reason that I avoided this horrible city. Our mother working at the Hemlock Medical Center took her from this world and nothing made me want to visit this place. Nothing.

Except Autumn.

Autumn was with my mom that night. She was also attacked and how we knew that my mother was leaving work. My mom spent most of her life working at the hospital, giving her time to the sick, and being the caregiver everyone needed. Very rarely did she ever get it in return. But Autumn tried.

Which was insane because she was just a child herself. Not an actual child, she was a senior in high school. The stories about this town were just that, stories. But Autumn swore they were true when I finally had the courage to talk to her. The detective on the case told me that Autumn was walking past the back of the hospital entrance when she heard my mother scream.

At just seventeen, she ran towards the cries and screams but didn't get there in time. The person who attacked my mom turned on Autumn and tried to kill the only witness to the crime.

I'll never forget going into her hospital room and seeing

her hooked up to the machines. She looked like she should have been dead. How she survived after all this time is a miracle. I hadn't given her much thought about making it, truthfully.

I wanted nothing to do with this town or anything about that night. Reliving that pain was awful, even now.

But after hearing her name, I had to do something. I felt compelled. After searching on the internet and in the police database, it wasn't hard to find Autumn and what became of her. According to her social media, she was head of the high school PTA, had two kids and looked just as young as I remembered her.

Maybe it was my subconscious telling me what to do, but I found myself driving on Lanier Drive, conveniently right outside of the high school. There were cars in the parking lot, and I could tell from the time of day, it wasn't the students' cars. Seemed it was my luck to stumble onto a PTA meeting.

If Willa Sims really had connected with my mother, this is the logical next step. To go see the woman who tried to save my mother's life.

I pulled my car into the parking lot and found an empty space relatively close to the front. Every part of this seemed insane, but I had managed to come this far. No sense in stopping now. There was a strange sensation traveling up my spine as I stepped out of the vehicle and started walking towards the entrance of the high school. Typically, I wasn't a self-conscious person, but today it felt like everyone was watching me. The men and women standing outside of the doors stopped talking as I approached. I smiled at them, pulled open the door and walked inside. I was an officer, a sheriff, there was nothing for me to shy away from.

That's when I heard the voices traveling through the foyer. The parents were meeting in the assembly hall off to my right. I slipped inside and sat at the back of the auditorium. I would recognize Autumn anywhere. Even from a hundred yards away. I couldn't get over how young she looked, even in person with no filters to help the photographs. All I could do was sit and listen.

"The prom committee meets next week to finalize the plans for our seniors. Remember, we have to finish the food prep and the DJ. Mary Sue is going to head up the decorating committee. Feel free to reach out if you want to help with any of this."

The room started to applause and Autumn signaled silence with her hand.

"And let's not forget the most important business we have to settle at the next official meeting. This is my last year serving the PTA. A replacement needs to be nominated and voted on next month. As much as I don't want to leave, my time to serve has lapsed."

Another round of applause erupted, and this time, people started standing. I could tell she was loved by the community of parents and somehow that put me at ease knowing she must have become a good individual. Even considering how badly she was hurt so many years ago.

"Thank you everyone, meeting adjourned."

As the people started to file out of the room, I stood up and walked opposite the flow of footsteps to approach Autumn.

"Good afternoon, officer. Can I help you?"

"Hi, Autumn. I'm sure you don't remember me. But I remember you."

"I'm sorry, no. I don't remember you. What's your name?"

My breath caught for a moment before I started to speak again. "Jacobs. Timothy Jacobs."

There was no hiding the look on her face. She knew my name, and I watched as a light went off in her mind as to where she knew me from.

"Oh," she sighed. "Oh I'm so sorry."

"Autumn," someone called from the other side of the stage.

She looked at the person calling her name and then back at me. I could tell she wanted to talk, but was torn.

"Go, I'll go wait in my vehicle outside. I'd like to talk to you when you have a minute."

Autumn nodded her head, "I'd like to talk too."

CHAPTER 3

LOCATION: HEMLOCK VALLEY HIGH SCHOOL —
TIMOTHY

*P*art of what I enjoyed doing as an officer was people-watch. Tonight, as I waited for Autumn to finish her meeting, I watched everyone flow from the school and walk to their cars. So many of the women didn't seem to pay attention to what was going on around them. There was no situational awareness happening. And maybe that was what happened the night my mother was killed. Why should women have to constantly be on guard? They should be able to stroll to their cars, take a break from work, or stand outside of a hospital without needing police protection.

I must have drifted off into my own mind, because the knocking on the window startled me. I jumped and looked to the right and saw Autumn's face just outside of the glass. I quickly got out of the vehicle and walked around the front of the car, and smiled at her.

"Officer Jacobs," she said in her sweet tone.

"Call me Timothy. Please."

She nodded. "Okay, Timothy, what did you want to talk about?"

My hand came up to my head, and I ran it through my hair. "So much," I said as I sighed. "Can I take you for a drink somewhere?"

"If you want, we can head into town and get something at Cherrie's Café."

A shiver went up my spine thinking about what had happened not too long ago in that town square at the book-shop. "Is that the only place?"

She nodded, "Small town, Officer, not much in the way of options."

"Can I drive you?" I wasn't even sure why I asked that. She was at the school. Surely, she had her car there.

"Actually, yes, I walked, so that would be nice."

My eyes lit up at her acceptance. "Allow me to get the door for you." I reached over and opened the passenger door to my cruiser. "It's not much, but it's my chariot."

I closed the door and then jogged to the other side and slipped into my driver's side seat. "Music?"

"Whatever you're listening to will be fine."

"I'm actually not much for music in the car. I was just being polite."

Autumn laughed, "Then silence is golden."

I couldn't help myself, I was grinning at her cheesy joke. I pulled out of the school parking lot and made my way down Lanier drive until Autumn spoke up.

"Here, turn right on W. Jasmine Drive. It will take us to the café."

Following her directions, I made the turn and passed the courthouse, the town sheriff's office, a real estate place, and an art museum. This place seemed way too small for an art museum. I parked the car outside of the café on the curb, got out, and walked around to open the door.

"I think I'm actually hungry, too."

Autumn grinned. "I am always hungry."

We walked into the café, and I saw a booth in the corner that looked like it would give some privacy. We both took our seats and pulled out the menu that was pressed against the wall on the table.

"What do you suggest here?" I looked over at the different sandwiches they had.

"Anything you pick, you will enjoy. I always do."

I noticed that the waitress was already walking up to us. I smiled as she approached the table.

"Hey there, Autumn, who is your friend here?"

"Jessica, this is Officer Jacobs. He's just passing through town. Thought I would give him a tour of the best café in the state."

"Damn straight we are. Welcome Officer. Today's meal is on the house. We support our LEOs."

"You don't have to do that, but thank you," I smiled at the woman.

"Jess, I'll take my usual, thanks."

She nodded at Autumn, "You want ground meat in it this time or just the cheese?"

"Just cheese, thanks."

"And for you?" Jessica turned her attention towards me.

"Give me a cheeseburger with a side salad. I'm watching my figure."

Both women laughed and then Jessica said, "Coming right up."

As she walked away, I couldn't help feeling nervous. I didn't know what I wanted to start with, but I knew the ball was in my court.

"You became a cop." Autumn said it as a declaration of fact, which made sense since I was a cop.

"Yeah, mom's murder was hard on me. I wanted to prevent others from going through what I did."

"I'm sorry you lost her so young."

"Thanks." I paused, thinking about how to say the next words. "I didn't know you survived. I honestly just found out this afternoon."

"How did you find me so quickly, then?"

It was my turn to grin. "I'm a cop, remember?"

She laughed, "Kind of scary what technology can do."

"I'll tell you the story, but you're going to think it's crazy. Just like I do."

"Okay, try me. What happened?"

How much of what I went through did I want to even share? Because it did make me sound crazy believing them.

"This morning, we got a call that Willa Sims needed to talk to me. Dispatch sent me the address, and I showed up, honestly, not long ago."

"Oh, I know Willa, this should be good."

"Yeah, okay, so you may believe this is crazy then." I chuckled. "Hey, we forgot to order drinks." I started looking around and then waved Jessica down.

"What can I do for you?"

"Can I get a Cherry Coke?" I always enjoyed those when I was off the clock, and this felt like a good time to get one.

"Sure thing!"

"Thanks." I said before turning my attention back to Autumn. "Now where was I?" Pausing to think about where I left off. "Oh yeah, Willa. So, I showed up to the bookstore and went in to take whatever statement was needed. She is not all there. Willa tried to convince me that my dead mother's spirit made her call me. And my dead mother's spirit told me through her that you were still alive."

"That's quite the story," Autumn nodded in agreement.

"I know. And here you are, alive. So does that mean Willa is talking to my dead mother?" There was a look on Autumn's face that told me she wanted to say something but was holding back her thoughts. "Just say whatever it is."

"She's telling the truth. That, I am sure. She never lies."

"Well, that's going to make this even more weird. When I found out what you do at the school, I decided to come find you. And saying this out loud makes me seem like a creep."

"Well, you're someone who wants answers. That's understandable. Maybe I can give them to you. What's your question?"

Jessica walked up with my soda in one hand and a tray of food in the other. We stopped talking as she set out my burger in front of me, the salad off to the side and a bowl of queso with chips in front of Autumn.

"That's your usual?" I asked.

Both women laughed and Autumn said, "Oh yeah. I really love cheese."

As Jessica walked away, I took a bite of my burger and then began to formulate my question.

"You look so young."

"Is that the question or a compliment?" Autumn asked.

"Both, I think. How have you not aged hardly at all since that tragic day?"

"Before I answer that, tell me what you know about Hemlock Valley." Autumn started dipping her chip into the cheese and biting into it. She looked like she was in total bliss as she savored the flavors.

"Not much. I avoid this place as much as I can. Just something about it that makes me get all out of sorts when I have to come out here, ever."

"Means you have good instinct. Most people assume it's a joke, just for sales and tourism. But if you live here, you know it's real. Our town is made up of creatures of the night."

Shaking my head back and forth, "I knew you were going to say that. And what, next you're going to say you look so young because you haven't aged, that you're a vampire?" I started laughing.

The curl in Autumn's lips told me that I didn't want to

know the answer. I took another bite of my burger and tried to change the subject.

"So, you're in charge of the PTA. How many kids do you have?"

"Nice topic avoidance. One, and he's a senior."

For some reason, I was scared to bring anything else up. I quietly ate my burger and when she was done with her chips and dip, I signaled for Jessica to come back.

"What else can I get you?"

"Just the check. Thank you, Jessica."

"Again, it's on the house. Thank you for your service."

Autumn smiled. "There is no arguing with her. Come on Timothy, let me show you around."

CHAPTER 4

LOCATION: HEMLOCK VALLEY CENTER OF TOWN — AUTUMN

Sitting across from someone who I hadn't seen in so many years was a bit surreal. His mother had saved my life in the end. Guilt had always been part of my memory of that night and one of the main reasons I never sought to find out more about him. The idea that he was partially orphaned because of me was a lot to handle. Especially considering how I ended up surviving.

But here we were, enjoying a meal. We had shared some laughs and some awkward moments. But when he asked me about my son, it made my guilt feel enhanced. My son still had a mother. By the time Timothy was my David's age, his mother had been taken from him. Now he was asking questions and making observations that required an open-minded answer. Discussing it in the café wasn't an option. My Sire didn't want any possibility of his identity being leaked. There was only one solution: we had to leave the café.

In response to my suggestion, his smile looked genuine as

it formed on his face. Something that, at times, was missing from our little town. So much of what we did here was an act for the tourists. It was refreshing to see this side of humanity.

"Where are you going to take me?" Timothy started walking to his cruiser.

"Right there." I reached my hand out and waited for him to take it.

"Here?"

I nodded, "Trust me, Officer Jacobs."

When our hands interlocked, I felt it. There was no denying he felt it, too. The surge of energy. His mother had been a witch, and he was one too. Even if he didn't realize it. He had raw, untapped magic flowing through his veins, and it was an intoxicating sensation until he let go of my hand.

"Did you feel that?" He asked the question with such an astonishing sense of surprise.

All I could do was smile, "Come on, follow me."

Weaving through cars and in and out of traffic, I gave an easy stroll across N. Lily Street until finding myself in the center of town. I walked across the park grass and sauntered into the beautiful gazebo. Taking a seat on the side of the wall, I wiggled my finger at Timothy and grinned. "Don't leave me here alone."

"Yes, ma'am." He chuckled and quickly joined me. "So, this is it? You wanted to show me this excellent wood construction?"

Giggling, I shook my head. "No, I wanted to sit in the middle of this beautiful town and tell you some of her secrets."

"I see," he said softly.

Reaching my hand over to his, once again I felt the jolt of energy. It was very real. "You like to get your haircut at barber shops?" I asked.

"Super Cuts works for me. Never been to a barber."

"What a shame. You will have to check out Frank

Grimes's shop over there on S. Pedal Lane one day. I think you and he would get along great."

"Is that part of the story you are going to tell me? The barber shop?"

I nodded, "Yes. But first. I want to tell you about your mother."

Timothy tried to pull his hand back, but I held onto it, I wasn't going to let him get away that quickly. "Trust me, this is hard enough being in the town where she died. I don't need to hear more about that night."

"What did Willa tell you that your mother said? Aside from me being alive."

"She wanted me to solve her murder. I just can't see why she said that. My mother was killed by a druggie that was lurking around the hospital. The sheriff's office told my dad that."

"Did you tell Willa?"

Timothy shook his head, "No. I don't think I even thought about it when the conversation was happening. It was too overwhelming talking to her about something so painful. It seemed like a cruel joke."

"I don't think it was a joke. Willa is a very powerful psychic witch. She wouldn't have exposed herself to you like that if she didn't have a real reason to."

Timothy tried to pull away again, but this time I let my fingers tease him. It seemed to help calm his nerves.

"Autumn, it's appearing as if you're holding back something. What aren't you really telling me?"

I sighed. "Let's start with the basics. Do you know the town's tourist lure?"

He nodded. "All of our towns around here have them. Thank you, Salem, for making tourism that much harder. Now we all have to have a gimmick. Your town pretends to be full of magical creatures."

"Good," I nodded, "this will make things easier. What if I

told you Mayor Thompson has a unique bubble around us to help keep us all safe? And, in fact, everything you think is a gimmick is actually reality?"

Timothy barked out a laugh, "I would say you and that Willa chick need your heads examined."

I grinned. "Ask me again why I look so young."

He turned to look at me, our bodies squared off. I now held each of his hands in one of mine and I was doing my best to give off the innocent, girl next door vibes.

"Ask me, Officer."

Timothy sighed, "Okay, I'll bite. Autumn, why do you look so young after all these years?"

"I'm a vampire."

I expected him to laugh or deny it. Instead, he sat there in silence for a moment. "Prove it."

This was unexpected, a treat that I rarely heard about. A brave soul who would be silly enough to ask a vampire that. Lucky for Officer Timothy, I wasn't big into killing. I loved the exchange of fluids. In fact, I relished it.

"Come closer, lean in." I told him.

His body leaned forward, our eyes didn't unlock for a few moments. I could feel my fangs elongating in my mouth and when he was at just the right distance, I broke eye contact, pushed my head down and my lips found his neck.

At first, I just kissed him. There was nothing more delightful than feeding on a man who was aroused. I could smell his hormones surging as my tongue teased his epidermis. Right when I thought he would pull away, I opened my mouth and bit into his neck.

Delicious copper blood spilled into my mouth. With each pull on his life, his warm salvation filled my body. I could feel my own pheromones start to release. My sex drive was being triggered and if I didn't stop soon, there would be no other options than to make love to this officer of the law, right here in public.

"Oh, God," Timothy moaned.

That was my cue to stop. I opened my mouth, retracted my fangs, and sealed his wound with a lick of my tongue. In a few short moments, there would be no evidence of what I had just done.

"So, you see, sometimes you can believe the rumor mills." I sat back, looking over at this sexy man sitting beside me.

"That was amazing," he said in a whispered tone.

I nodded. "It was. Do you want more of it?"

It was the grin on his face that told me "yes." I stood up, pulled on his hand and grinned, "Come with me to The Attic, right over there. It's a vampire bar. I know the owner. He won't mind if I give you a little more in one of the back rooms."

~

TIMOTHY

I wasn't sure what had me more enthralled, how sexy she looked, or the fact that I was hard as a rock and in desperate need of release. I let Autumn guide me across the rest of the park until we got to E. Dalia Street. There, we made our way into this club that had no openings to the outside world. Everything was concealed and suddenly my cop instinct started to kick in. It was almost as if she had a spell on me before and now reality was breaking through.

"Autumn, maybe we shouldn't."

"Don't back out now," she said as she pulled open the door and quickly brought us inside. The club was quiet. I expected music to be blasting, but instead it was a calm classical number playing lightly in the background.

Autumn walked up to the bartender and spoke to her. I watched the woman point in a certain direction and Autumn followed it with her head turning. Then she nodded and turned around, came to me, grabbed my hand and said, "Come."

I had no willpower to refuse.

We were now sitting in a secluded corner, on a U-shaped couch that was the most comfortable leather I had ever sat on.

"Do you want to finish what we started outside?" Autumn's voice was seductive in this setting.

"I want nothing more than that." My response was truthful. I wanted this woman, and I had no idea why I needed her so badly. I pulled her closer to me, leaned in, kissed her and suddenly time slowed to a standstill. It was just her and I, no one else in the world mattered.

I felt her hands under my shirt. I hadn't even noticed her pulling it out of my pants. Then I realized my gun was still on me and it was as if we shared a thought because she whispered, "it's okay, I'll move it," right before she pulled it out of its holster and slid it into a cubby below us on the outside of the couch.

There was so much about this situation that was, for lack of a better word, insane, but I didn't want to stop. I let her remove the rest of my belt and place it all in the same slot. She soon had the buttons on my shirt opened and I felt her fingers teasing my skin on the places the bullet-proof vest didn't cover.

"This looks hot on you." She declared.

I didn't want to be dominated; it was my turn to change the table on her. Shifting positions, now I was on top of her, looking down into her perfect eyes. My hands traveled down her body, exploring her every inch. Piece by piece I undressed her and soon I was looking at the most delectable afternoon delight I could have dreamt up. "Oh, my," I spoke.

Autumn's smile warmed me and as her legs fell open, my body went on instinct. I moved to the honeycomb of her warmth and licked my tongue across her slit. She was an intoxicating masterpiece, and I needed her. My tongue dove inside her folds. She was already moist, ready for me to conquer her. I found her hooded button of pleasure and slowly began familiarizing myself with her moans. They would alternate as I pressed against it with my nose at first, then flicked it with my tongue. But the real joy was when I took it between my teeth and lightly bit down, applying the slightest pressure.

Her hips rocked, and the fountain of juices that started to flow endlessly from her told me I hit the jackpot. I needed to finish this claiming. I needed to take her. My hands struggled to release my pants. I was too caught up in the moment, but soon my cock was free, and I was teasing her slit once more.

"May I?" The question seemed a little too late but the gentleman inside of me made me ask it.

"Make love to me, Officer Jacobs!"

Her words pushed me from desire to claiming in an instant. My cock dove into her warmth and my god was it perfect. It was as if she was made for me. Her walls wrapped around my cock like the perfect glove. Custom-built just for its owner.

Thrusting in and out, I couldn't help the overwhelming sensations taking over. My arms wrapped around her shoulders, and I started vigorously pumping into her. Harder and harder with each thrust. I felt like an animal in need of dominating and nothing was going to hold me back.

When Autumn leaned towards me, I thought she was going to kiss me, but instead she went for my neck again. And when she bit down this time, something happened.

I erupted inside of her. My cock unleashed my pent up load of cum that had been stirring inside of me all day long. It was the most sensational experience. When we were done, my body was drained, and I couldn't find the desire to move from that spot.

"Wow," she said.

"Yeah, ditto," I murmured.

"It's been a while since I had sex with a wizard. That was incredible."

My mind was spinning, so it took me a moment to focus on what she had just said. But when I played it back, my reaction wasn't what it should have been. "A wizard? You sure you're not the one who put the spell on me?"

She laughed. "Officer Jacobs, I need you to come home with me. I have a lot to tell you."

"In a minute, I think I want to stay like this, just a little bit longer." I nuzzled her neck and bit at her skin. Her breasts were under my bullet-proof vest and when I tried to find them, I realized I was still partially dressed. "Oh, maybe we should go to your place. I'm sure I look ridiculous."

Autumn smiled, ran her hand through my hair and said, "You look very hot and sexy."

I didn't respond to her with words, just with the passionate kiss I gave her. Something inside of me changed this afternoon, and I wasn't sure what it was.

CHAPTER 5

LOCATION: AUTUMN'S HOME — AUTUMN

Timothy drove me to my home just past Shifters Lane. I wasn't sure if he knew the different obligations that came with being a creature of the night, since I was confident he didn't know he was a wizard. But as he pulled into my driveway, I decided now was as good of time as any to start explaining things.

"Do you like tea?" I asked as we walked to the front door?"

He nodded, "Yes I do."

"Great, I'll make you some. Come on in and get comfortable in the living room. My son's not expected home from football practice for a while. We will have some time alone."

I went into the kitchen, grabbed two cups, and then added water to the kettle. As it began to boil, I set the tea bags in each cup and then called out, "Do you want any sugar?"

"Sure, thanks."

The water was at the right piping hot temperature in the

kettle, so I began to pour it over the individual tea bags. Using a spoon to squeeze the tea and stir I assembled everything, grabbed the cups and walked into the living room.

"Before I get started, do you have any questions I need to answer first," I set his cup down in front of him on the coffee table, then joined him on the couch.

"I do, actually."

Nodding, "Okay, hit me."

"Were you a vampire when my mom died?"

This was an easy start to the conversation, "No. I was pretty much a human teenager in the wrong place at the wrong time. The truth about what happened, is that your mom saved my life."

"I didn't know that," he said softly.

My head moved up and down, "Yeah, that was left out of the papers. My parents were Fae's and somehow managed to have a human child. Which was fine, they loved me. But it made me the target of a lot of hazing many years ago. Which was how I ended up in the hospital."

"Did my mom treat you or something?"

I shook my head, "No. I was going to get an exam because some fae girls had hurt me, but I decided against it because I didn't want the law involved. That would have made life worse. I was walking home, taking the ally as a shortcut when a werewolf came out of nowhere."

"Seriously?" He looked shocked.

Nodding my head, "Yeah. It had white foam all over his mouth. It was clear that he had been laced with some drugs. I started to run and scream but he grabbed a hold of me. My leg was pretty mangled up and I was wailing in pain when your mom showed up."

"Is that who killed her then?"

My eyelids lowered and I took a sip of my tea, "Yes. But not before she saved me. She casted protection and healing spells over my body. The pain of my leg being mended was almost unbearable. But she ended up keeping me alive long enough for the coroner to arrive. Everyone thought I was dead, but he took me back and saved me. By changing me into a vampire."

"That's a really extreme story. It's like I want to believe you because you did just drink my blood. But my mind wants to call B.S. on all of this."

I nodded, "I get it. But there is more that you need to know."

"Like, the whole part where my mother cast some type of spell on?."

"Yes," I said, "that." I took another drink of the tea and kept talking. "There was something about her spell that didn't wear off. My body kept trying to rejuvenate itself constantly. That's why I can walk in the sun and others, like those at The Attic, can't. They need powerful rings from the mayor in order to sun walk."

"You sound like some crazy vampire novel or movie," he lowered his head into his hand and started rubbing his temple.

"Do you want me to stop?'

"No, what happened to the monster who killed her?"

"I was told that Sheriff Jackson showed up with his pack and they ripped him apart."

"Then, if they know who really killed my mother, why did my mom tell me I needed to solve her murder?"

My shoulders lifted and fell in a shrug, "Maybe it wasn't so much about solving the crime as uncovering the truth. Because the truth exposes your own life and who you are."

"Maybe. But I don't think I am anything like my mother."

I shook my head, "I can taste it in your blood. You have the gift, even if you never use it."

"This is a lot to uncover, and I don't know how to process all of it. My father died a year ago, so I can't even talk to him about it."

My hand reached over and took his, "I understand. But you don't have to be alone."

"I have another question," he asked as he squeezed my hand. "If you're a vampire, how do you have a kid?"

"Oh, that's easy. My parents were mated and when my father died, my mother died with him. My little brother was three at the time. I adopted him and am raising him as my son."

"Of all the insanity that has gone on today, that's the most believable part of all of this."

I laughed, "Yeah, that was pretty easy to explain."

"I'm going to need some time. I think I need to go."

"Okay, I hope you come back." I said, feeling a lot of disappointment that he would be leaving.

"I hope I do too."

$\approx$

LOCATION: AS THE EMERALD TURNS

TIMOTHY

After leaving Autumn's I had every intention of heading home. When I passed by the town square and saw the bookstore front looking back at me, I knew I needed to go back inside and finish what was started. I parked my car, got out and walked up to the door, pulling it open.

"Officer Jacobs, I knew you would be back." Willa said from behind the register.

"This was a very odd day, Ms. Sims."

"Do you want to go sit back down?" She started to move out from behind the checkout counter.

I shook my head, "No. I just have a simple question."

She nodded, "Okay, what is it?"

"You said you were talking with my mother. If that's true,

what was the nickname she gave me as a baby? Only she would know this."

Willa chuckled, "Is this really what you need, in order to believe everything you learned today, Officer Jacobs?"

"Yes," I said nodding.

I watched as Willa closed her eyes, mumbled something to herself, smiled and then opened her eyes looking at me with so much warmth.

"She called you, her miracle."

My heart stopped, I couldn't breathe and now I knew everything that had happened today was 100% true.

CHAPTER 6

LOCATION: AUTUMN'S HOME — AUTUMN

*W*atching Timothy walk away after explaining everything that had happened was hard. I wanted to be there to comfort him and help him find his closure. But when I heard the engine of a car pulling into my driveway, my thoughts started to race. He was back. I didn't know where he had gone but he had been gone for an hour. I looked myself over in the mirror and walked towards my door, when I heard his hand knocking on the outside. Smiling, I opened the door and looked at the handsome, chiseled man looking back at me.

"Officer Jacobs, can I help you?" I noticed he had changed clothes and wasn't wearing his bullet proof vest anymore.

"Yeah, I think we have some unfinished business left." He stepped across the threshold and then shut the front door. "When's your son getting home?"

"Not for another hour or so probably."

"Good," Timothy said as he rushed me, wrapped his arms around my body and kissed my lips.

~

TIMOTHY

There was a weird sensation that overcame every part of my body. I needed her. I needed to be inside her and nothing would quench this thirst. When she opened the door, she looked magnificent, and I was going to ravish her right there on the threshold. Keeping myself composed long enough to hear when her son would be home was the best I could come up with. My hands explored her body as we stood there kissing.

My eyes opened and I saw an empty wall just behind us. I pushed our bodies together in the direction of that wall and when her back hit it with a thud, my cock jumped in anticipation. I started working my fingers over her stomach. Grabbing the hem of her shirt and pulling it over her head. Next was her bra. Then her pants. By the time I had her stripped of her clothes, she was naked as the day she was born, pressed between my hard body and the cold wall.

"You're so pretty," I said to her.

"Less talk, more of this," she said as her hands went to my pants and started working them open.

"Yes, ma'am."

I helped her along the path, stripping off my shirt and pushing my pants down. There we were, like animals in heat, in her foyer, naked and ready for carnal pleasure. My hands reached around and grabbed her butt cheeks. I pulled her up and she wrapped her legs around my hips. Balancing us together, my cock pressed inside of her as I roughly slammed her over and over against the wall.

This was it, the perfect moment. Savage, yet real, passionate, yet tamed. I was in control, and I knew what I wanted. I wanted nothing more than to dominate this beautiful blonde woman that stole my heart from inside me. The draw was unreal and somehow I had my mother to thank for all this.

I pulled my cock out from her and looked around, "There, that table." My arms wrapped around her body and held her against me as I carried her through the room and bent her over the table. Her ass was great. Nice and plump, perfect for spanking. My hand came down a few times on her creamy white cheek. Her yelps of approval told me to keep going. My dick slid back inside of her, this time at a different angle. Just like before, she fit like a glove.

Pounding away, my hands held onto her hips as I alternated spankings with my thrusts. When I was about to explode, I leaned further over, my arm reaching around her neck and my hand grabbing her throat.

"Tell me you're mine." I snarled into her ear. I wasn't sure what came over me, but there was an animal inside of me that needed to claim her like this.

"Yes, yes," she panted.

I leaned my mouth down and instead of kissing her sweet skin, I bit into it. I didn't have fangs like her, so I didn't break any skin. But I left my mark, and she yelped in delight.

The release that followed for both of us shook our bodies to our core and when we were done, we both collapsed on top of the table.

"Uhm, that was new for me." I said, panting and trying to catch my breath.

She chuckled, "Yeah, can't say I've done the mating thing with anyone before."

"Mating thing? You were a virgin?" I sat up in shock. "I'm so sorry!"

Autumn laughed, "No, not that kind of mating. I've had sex. This kind of mating, where you claimed me. That's not something I've ever done before. And you did that on instinct."

I shrugged. "No clue what I was doing. I was just in the moment. It is like you have a wicked spell on me."

She kept laughing. "I have placed the spell when you're the wizard?"

I nodded, "Told you, not a wizard, so yes you have the spell."

"If you're not a wizard, then why do we both have a mating mark on our shoulder where you bit me?"

As her words processed in my head, I looked down at my shoulder and then hers. There was a marking there that, in fact, wasn't there before.

"Oh my God," I mumbled.

"Well, guess you are magical now too, aren't you."

Our eyes locked, and I didn't know what to say or do. I felt overwhelmed with emotion and questions. This afternoon had suddenly taken a deep shift into forever and ever and I didn't even know what to say.

"It's okay, Timothy. We will get through this together."

There was only one thing left to do with an answer like that. I cupped her face in my hands, leaned over, and kissed her. Our lips were one and together they began to learn all about one another in a slow and meticulous way.

"You up for round 3?" she asked as she felt my cock starting to harden again.

I grinned, "Absolutely.

≈

LOCATION: AS THE EMERALD TUNS

RAVEN BURKE

"I told you, Raven, he would be back." Willa said, as I was cleaning up the magazine rack.

"But you shouldn't have unlocked his powers without

telling him how to use them." I was always the more practical partner in all of this.

"He's with Autumn. She is a strong vampire. I'm not worried." Willa shrugged off my concerns.

I shook my head at her and then started wiggling my finger. "I'm telling you, one day, your meddling will come back to bite you in the ass. You better be careful, Willa."

Shrugging it off, she smiled. "Today's not that day, sister. Let's enjoy another successful mating in this town with a nice dance in the woods."

I laughed, "You go have your naked moonlight dance. I got a hot date."

"Oh, you do?" Willa perked up.

"I do, with Mark."

Willa rolled her eyes, "Which Mark? Hot Mark I hope!"

I laughed again, "Yes hot Mark from the bank. I gotta start working on my 401K you know."

"Atta girl," Willa cheered. You go enjoy your night. And make sure you do everything I would do!

My hand lifted up and waved to my best friend goodbye. "Stay away from the leaves with three! We don't want another poison ivy repeat!

Willa burst into laughter, "We're not twelve anymore. I know which ones to avoid!"

"Thank the gods. See you tomorrow!" I walked out of the store and down the road towards the bank.

One really never knew what was in store for this little town of ours.

he End

HEMLOCK VALLEY

TAKEN BY THE VAMPIRE

SUNNY A MORGAN

CHAPTER 1

ONYX

I stood at the edge of the cliff, mesmerized by the valley below. I had grown tired; maybe I should take the plunge and end it, once and for all. No one was left to take care of, but with my luck, it would just paralyze me, leaving my life even more pathetic. The crunching sound of the dirty day old snow beneath my boots echoed in my ears as I wondered, what if I just did it? Forget it all and end it. Maybe a sunlit suicide.

The icy icy wind howled around me, too bad it could not numb away all my thoughts.

As a vampire, I was born in the protector class. I was descended from a long line of powerful vampires. Surpassing most supernatural beings, including my brethren, my strength was unmatched, and my life seemed endless.

I am half millennia, and I have lost the desire for life. It's not that I particularly wanted to die, but the thought of living my life alone had become tiring. I used to live for the fight. The fight to protect the innocent beings in the world.

Humans, with their free will, have become a society of hatred and disorder. At times, the mortals did things more disgusting than the demons I hunted.

I felt Slater step up next to me, disturbing my thoughts.

"I am not in the mood to clean up your guts today. Do us both a favor and jump when someone else is hunting with you." My oldest friend said as he clasped my shoulder.

In the diminishing light of early evening, the Egyptian markings that covered Slater's arms seemed to almost glow against his dark skin.

I glared at Slater, jerking from his grasp. "Stop reading my fucking mind. You know that pisses me off."

Slater grinned the action not fully reaching his eyes, but then again Slater never genuinely smiled. "You're always pissed off. If I could block all those fucked up thoughts in your head, I would, but right now you are projecting way too much for me not to hear you loud and clear."

My scowl deepened, and I stepped back from the edge of the mountain. Frustrated and maybe relieved, I hadn't taken the plunge before Slater started his bitching. Even more annoyed because I knew that the fall would not wipe me out.

The fact that Slater felt the need to babysit me did not help my foul mood. I was not sure when the depression set in or when I became so angry at everything, but still I did not need someone watching over me like I was some nut case who would flip out at any moment. I could still do my job and do it well.

"She wasn't meant for our life, Onyx. Her decision was made. She chose Lucian, let her go," Slater muttered, the twinge of bitterness not hidden in his voice.

I turned on Slater, my amber eyes glowing. "DON'T! Don't you fucking speak of my sister like she was disposable," I snarled.

"I know this is hard for you to see, but Angelica is gone." Slated sighed.

"You loved her once and now you act like she was nothing. How can you be so heartless?" I snapped.

Slater's eyes narrowed in on me. "You have no fucking idea how heartless I can be, old friend. Trust me, you don't want to know how deep my cruel nature actually is." Slater's chest heaved, growling through clenched teeth.

Our eyes met, locked on one another. We were about the same size, both well over six feet and about two hundred and fifty pounds of pure muscle. Both had pale skin color, but that's where our similarities ended. I had dark brown hair and amber-colored eyes that, until recently, held a flicker of humor and mischief.

Slater had shoulder length dark blonde hair with golden green eyes. His eyes sparked with knowledge, power, and hatred. A deadly combination for anyone who crossed him.

I was not afraid of Slater; I respected his abilities and typically would not push him, but I wanted a fight today. Rather than my old friend, I would have preferred to fight Lucian. But tonight Slater might have gotten the honor, except the asshole, would probably let me win because he felt pity for me.

"You are not the only one who lives in regret," Slater said as he stepped closer to me. "The rage you think you can not release does not have to continue to strangle you. But you will have to accept your fate and leave the past behind."

"Stop reading my mind and take your own advice and leave me the hell alone." Onyx retorted.

Rage and self-hatred warmed my blood. I pushed past Slater and stormed off. A fight was what I needed, and I needed it fast. I made it about fifty yards into trees leading toward the forest before I heard the animalistic sounds. Demons. My head darted up as I took a deep breath. Just ahead to my left, three demons stalked through the trees.

"Finally." A small grin formed on my face. The first time in weeks I felt excited. I needed this fight. All three were easily a foot taller than me, with broad shoulders and thickly muscled arms and legs. Already in their demonic forms, they must have been hunting.

My smile widened at the sight of them. "Hey, dumbasses, do you want to play?"

The demons turned their red gazes toward me. The one in the middle growled, his voice thick and distorted. "Three against one. You should probably start running."

My head fell back on my shoulders as the sound of my laughter rang through the forest. "Not a chance," I smirked, my lips curved into a smile. "Are you just going to stand there admiring my beauty? Or are you actually going to move? Or are you trying to scare me with your looks?"

The three demons spread out in a V formation, crouched, ready to attack. "You three must be part of Lucian's ugly brigade. Is that how you defeat your enemies?" Slater smirked, coming up behind me.

I was disappointed when I heard Slater, but decided to just go with it. "Yeah, they sure could scare a lesser man to death with their looks."

Slater reached for his dagger. "I'll take big bad and scary on the left and you can have dumb and dumber."

"I'll take all of them. You can watch in case they have a backup around," I ordered.

"Not a chance, friend," Slater protested.

"Stay back unless I need you," I growled.

Shaking his head, Slater leaned against a tree. "All yours jackass. Good luck boys, it looks like my friend is in a fighting mood."

"Come on, fuckers. Let's get this party started." With a roar, I charged.

CHAPTER 2

SIX MONTHS LATER

ONYX

It had been an unusually quiet night, and the streets were empty. Not the norm on the weekends in Hemlock Valley. I strode down the deserted town square. The quiet enfolded me. It was both comforting and disconcerting. I was reassigned to this small town in the states about six months ago. I hated this assignment. Nothing but human tourist filled the streets of this little town with supernatural beings.

I had never seen so many creatures getting along in my long life. It was strange, and I wasn't sure if I would ever get used to it.

Most nights I walked the streets and guided tourists to the Attic. A local club with a bit more spice than the other local businesses. Tonight, the streets were empty, and I was just about to call it a night when I stopped dead in my tracks, shock ripping through me. I felt something I haven't felt in months, not since Angelica left with Lucian. But at this moment, I felt heartache and fear. Someone else's emotions, a female.

I saw a demon attacking a female. The woman cried and begged for the demon to take her purse and leave. But the demon wasn't interested in her money. The demon seemed to gain strength from this female's fear.

Darting between buildings, I leaped into the large trees along the street, moving so quickly most mortals would not see me. I would just appear as a gust of wind, a blur.

"Stop that disgusting crying." The demon hissed at the female, artificially deepening his voice.

I burst from the trees and ran across a small parking lot in front of one of the restored historic buildings around the town square. I could not believe there was a demon here in Hemlock.

"Please," the female replied, "just take the money. Here's my purse. Take it."

"Do you not know what I am?" the demon asked, his voice almost seemed disappointed.

"Someone who is obviously on drugs." She countered. "Just take my purse and maybe we'll all get lucky and you'll overdose."

I almost laughed. The human may not know what the hell was happening, but she recovered from her confusion pretty quick. She was not buying the monster in front of her, as anything more than a kid hopped up on drugs.

"I don't want your money," the demon said resentfully. His eyes now turned red, and I saw the renewed fear in the woman's eyes.

"Let her go," I said through clenched teeth.

The demon pulled the woman closer to him. His body contorted into his demonic form. His nails grew into long talons, his shoulders widened, and when he peeled back his lips to snarl, his animal-like teeth gleamed.

The female's eyes widened. "Oh, fuck." She gasped.

I could do nothing to free the human until the demon released her. If I struck now, the demon could break her neck. So, I merely cleared my throat. The demon and the woman looked in my direction.

"Where the hell did you come from?" Spouted the demon, shifting his body to make sure I saw his captive.

The woman turned her head to meet my gaze. A strange little tickle floated through my chest. She had bright blonde hair that fell just above her hips, olive-colored skin, and large eyes that appeared to be azure. She looked both hopeful and fearful when she looked into my eyes.

The demon drew his lips farther back and hissed. Tearing me out of my trance, I crossed my arms over my chest and leaned against the building.

"Yeah — yeah, I know you are the big bad demon. But I'm the bigger, badder, vampire." I smiled widely, revealing my large fangs with an animalistic snarl.

"Fucking blood sucker, back the fuck off now before you die," the demon said.

My head flew back with my laughter, boisterous. "I see the brightest demons are out tonight."

"Look, it's apparent you two have some sort of male thing going on here and really there is no need for me." The woman spoke nervously. "How about you let me go and then you can go deal with that one?" She suggested to the demon.

"She's right, demon, let her go. We can settle this, and if you're as badass as you think you are, then you shouldn't have any trouble with me." I goaded.

The demon was distracted enough for the woman to stealthily grab something from her purse. Some sort of spray that she yanked out. Wasting no time, she sprayed the demon's eyes and mouth. With the demon momentarily distracted, I pulled two daggers out and threw them. One landed in the demon's chest, forcing him to release the female.

Not waiting to see where the other fell, I shot into action. Quick as lightning, I sliced the demon's carotid and brachial arteries, killing him instantly. The woman took this as her chance to run.

I wanted to make sure she was alright, but I could not leave the body on the street. Pulling out his cell, I called the sheriff's office for someone to clean up the mess.

"I broke up a demon trying to kill a woman at the Town Square. I need to get rid of the body, but I also need to find the woman. She ran off terrified." I explained.

"Yeah, I bet she ran. I'll be right there, but don't leave the body just in case tourist come by."

"The woman–," I started.

"Let her go. We can play it off as part of the town's paranormal experience." Deputy Walker said.

CHAPTER 3

ROSA

"*H*ey Rosa, snap out of it. Your table's ready to order." Lila yelled.

"Finally. I've already gone over there four times as they debated on which salad to get. Who orders a salad at a diner?" I snapped back.

"I didn't realize you didn't need your tips." Lila snorted as she strutted past me.

Truth to be told, I'm normally a great waitress. But my mind has been elsewhere all day. After last night and almost being killed by some asshole and the sexy man who saved me, my mind has been all over the place today.

I'm new to Hemlock Valley. My uncle Donald Sims insisted I move in with him after my mother passed away a couple of months ago. He got me the job at the diner and has been filling me in on this strangely unique little town.

Let me be clear, I am not foolish or believe in fairytales, but I believe in all the things that go bump in the night. Hemlock Valley was a haven for all those creatures. Examples, Cherrie, the owner of the diner, and her family were wolf shifters. The owners of the Attic were vampires, my uncles, and my family are human, but they possess unique gifts. My cousin Willa was psychic. Uncle Donald was a healer, and me, well, I'm just a human. You see, I was adopted into the family.

"ROSA!"

Crap, that was not Lila. That was Cherrie as in the diner's owner.

"Sorry, Cherrie. I'm going right over."

"Snap to it." She said, crossing her arms over her chest.

"Have we decided?" I asked the couple at my table.

"The meatloaf with mashed potatoes and green beans." The gentleman said.

"You're not getting a salad?" His companion asked.

"No. Sandra." He answered and sat back against the booth.

"Well, now I'm not sure what I want," Sandra said, her eyes scanning over the menu.

I took a deep breath and tried not to sound annoyed. "Why not get the salad and share some of his meatloaf?" I said with a wink.

"Oh, yes, good idea!" Sandra said. "Italian dressing, please."

"You got it." I smiled and dashed away from their table.

Two hours later, I was on my way to meet uncle Donald.

"Beautiful, girl!" Donald said, pulling me into a hug. "I found the most fabulous dress upstairs for you. You need a night out. Willa and Raven are going to the Attic's Valentine's Day party tomorrow and you are going, too."

"Actually, I already told Willa I would go." I said.

"Perfect. Now go try on the dress." Donald said. "You will be the bell of the ball."

"Thank you." I said as I raced up the stairs.

CHAPTER 4

ONYX

*T*he woman across the bar was meant for sex with her full red lips, captivating slightly slanted blue eyes were just a piece of her allure. Her white-blonde hair contrasting beautifully against her honeyed colored skin, and curves that would have a man salivating from miles away. I couldn't believe she was the scared woman from two nights ago. Tonight, she had all the sex appeal of a goddess.

She slowly walked toward me and, as cliché as it sounded, the sea of people seemed to part as she made her way toward the bar.

"Onyx, isn't it?" She said when she finally stood in front of me.

"Yes, and you are?" I asked, taking her hand and bringing it to my lips.

"Rosa." She replied.

"It's lovely to meet you."

"I wanted to thank you for saving me the other night." She said, as her lush lips curved into a smile.

I took my time to look fully at Rosa and was rewarded with a warm smile as the heavy bass pulsed around us, and lights flickered over her bare skin.

"Having fun?" she asked.

"I am now." I smirked.

Rosa smiled, a soft laugh escaping her red lips. I cocked my head, noting her strapless red dress designed to seduce.

"Do you have a date?" I asked.

She shook her head. "No. No, Valentine this year."

"Were you hoping to meet your Knight in Shining Armor tonight?" I asked.

"Maybe, my Blood in Shining Armor." She said, poorly imitating Dracula. "It is owned by vampires, after all."

"Maybe you already met yours." I added, stepping closer to her.

She blushed. "What is upstairs?" She asked, pointing to the crowd in front of the elevator.

"Upstairs is a private sex club. Still want to go up?" He inquired, his eyes narrowing on her. The upstairs part of the Attic specialized in sexual fetishes.

She chewed her bottom lip before she straightened her shoulders. "Yes. I've never been to a sex club before and something tells me you are the perfect guide."

She tossed her braided hair over her shoulder, the sophisticated weave landing just above her hips. Her taunting laugh caused my cock to pulse. She didn't wait for me to answer, but instead walked to the elevator.

"Another?" A raspy feminine voice asked. I turned away from the crowd and Rosa, to answer the female behind the bar.

She leaned forward, causing what had to be a deliberate display of her breasts. The black leather bustier did very little to cover her ample cleavage. I noticed the Eye of Re tattooed just above the curve of her right breast. My gaze glanced up into her gray eyes, outlined in black liner, framed by thick dark lashes.

"No, I'm leaving." I dropped cash on the bar when she grabbed my wrist. My eyes looked down at her olive-toned skin against my own pale skin. This female who probably had men hitting on her night after the night did nothing for me.

"She didn't seem interested." She quickly blurted out, talking about Rosa.

An attempt to make me jealous? I shook my head. "Not tonight." I gently but firmly removed the woman's hand from my wrist.

CHAPTER 5

ROSA

"**S**he's with me," Onyx told the bouncer.

"She's human." The bouncer countered.

"I'll take responsibility." Onyx said, his tone left no room for debate.

"Your balls." The bouncer said, handing Onyx a collar and leash before he removed the red velvet rope to allow us to pass.

"What did he mean your balls?" I asked, as Onyx led me through the crowd.

He smirked. "Humans aren't allowed upstairs. It can be too much of a temptation for the patrons."

"Maybe this was a bad idea." I said nervously.

"Oh, it is a bad idea." He chuckled.

Onyx stepped closer to me and held up the collar. "Still want to explore?"

My eyes widened at the collar. "Is that necessary?"

"Rules. On rare occasions, when a human is admitted upstairs, the collar, and leash are a must. It tells everyone she is taken. It should keep you safe from almost everyone." He leaned in and let his fangs graze my shoulder as he snapped the collar and leash in place. "Your guide is a vampire, after all."

Onyx's build was more of a shifter, broad and muscular, but everything screamed vampire. A strong jawline dusted with a five o'clock shadow, sculpted cheekbones, dark hair, piercing amber eyes, and, of course, sharp pointy fangs.

"You look beautiful tonight." He said. His voice was pure seduction, and it had heat swirling through my body.

"Thank you." I said.

"Let me get you a drink," he said.

"I should buy you a drink."

"Another time, perhaps." He nodded toward a half round booth.

"Do you have a private room here?" I asked.

There was something about Onyx that made me want to do things I never would have considered before. Such as have a one-night stand at a sex club. Call it a sexual bucket list of sorts.

ONYX

THE LITTLE HUMAN WAS TOO tempting. And she it seemed she wanted to play well. Who am I to disappoint?

"I do. Are you ready to play?" I asked.

"Yes." she whispered as I wrapped the leash around my hand several times.

I guided her back to the private room section of the club. There was a guard outside the hall of rooms. He handed me a key after showing him my VIP member card. We walked the short distance to the fourth room on the right. With the key, I unlocked the door. I stepped to the side and released my hold on the leash, allowing Rosa to walk freely through the door. I saw her approach the glass display cabinet filled with various toys and floggers. Approaching her, I wrapped an arm around her waist and pulled her close. She let out a surprised gasp, but didn't pull away.

"Are you sure you want to do this?" I whispered, letting my lips brush against the shell of her ear. "Rosa?" I said firmer when she did not answer.

"Yes, Onyx." She breathed, her voice throatily dusted with lust.

"Are you wet?" I asked.

"Yes." She moaned.

"Are you ready to learn about impact play?" I give her thigh a light smack.

"Yes,"

"Do you know about safe words?" I asked.

"Yes. Red. Stop. Yellow. Slow down. Green. Good to go."

"Perfect. If anytime you cannot say your safe words, tap my thigh."

"Okay." She nodded.

"Strip." I demanded.

She chewed her bottom lip momentarily before pulling her dress off her lovely body. No bra, just red lacy panties. She shimmied out of them. I stared at her in just her red heels. I wanted to fuck her with them on, but for my plans, they might be a hazard.

"On the spanking bench." I ordered. She turned and stared at me with confusion. I saw an array of emotions flicker in her pretty blue eyes. Rosa was around five foot seven, not too short and not too tall, perfect for me. She had lush curves and killer legs.

She stared at the bench but made no move to get into place. I prayed she didn't refuse me. I wanted her shackled and face down on the whipping bench, with her legs lewdly splayed on the sides of the seat. Her slick, intimate folds spread against the leather-covered wood. I wanted to paint her ass cheeks red with my kangaroo whip. In due time.

"The pain can lead you to pleasure beyond anything you've ever experienced before." I brushed my thumb over her cheekbone. "If it becomes too much, we'll stop. Just say red, and we'll stop, but try to take as much as you can."

"I want to try." She said with a sigh, and I felt my muscles relax.

"Straddle the bondage horse," I ordered. "Stretch your legs back to line up with the horse's legs and grip the front legs." I grinned as she struggled a little to follow my instructions. "Exquisite."

Pulling her closer, I grabbed her hips and slid her down the bench. I kneeled behind her, and my hand ran up the length of her leg and back down. I fastened the leather strap around her ankle, binding her to the horse. With all her limbs, I slowly repeated this action, leaving her tethered to the sawhorse.

I scanned the room. To start with, I should use a beginner's flogger or paddle. I wanted my handprint to redden her ass. Tomorrow, I wanted her to feel my handprint. I massaged and kneaded her upturned ass. Her ass was perfection.

"Are you ready?" I waited for an answer, but it was fucking hard. My hand was itching to spank her ass.

"Yes." She moaned.

CHAPTER 6

ROSA

I couldn't believe I was straddling a spanking bench, with my limbs strapped and the most vulnerable parts of my body exposed to a vampire I just met. I closed my eyes, and my hands gripped the legs of the bench as I steadied myself for his hand. My breath left my lungs the second his hand touched my right ass cheek. The loud sound of his hand landing on my skin echoed through the room. Another smack followed, then another, and another. He built a rhythm alternating between my ass cheeks. I thought he would have me count, but he didn't demand a number. I counted silently, anyway. Fifteen times his hand landed on my ass.

My body was reeling; I felt like shots of electrical energy were coursing through my veins. But with Onyx spanking me, it was like something awakened. My body was reacting. I could feel my juices dripping down my thighs. Twenty times, his hand landed on my ass, and he still continued. My ass and pussy were on fire.

Would he fuck me? I wanted him to fuck me, ram his cock into my pussy and claim it. I didn't even know this man, but I wanted him inside me more than my next breath. His hand picks up speed, and he lands another five smacks on my skin.

"Perfect."

Tears ran down my cheeks as I tried to calm myself and even my breath. Onyx quickly unfastened the straps, and my body sagged against the bench. I wasn't sure what to do now. I didn't think I could move if I wanted to, but what was the protocol after letting a stranger spank you twenty-five times?

"You did so well," he whispered, his hand striking my skin. I gasped when I felt his thick finger slip into my pussy. "Fuck, Rosa, you're drenched."

I hissed when he pulled his finger from my cunt. I missed it instantly.

"That was —" I started, but I had no words to describe it. He picked me up and carried me to the bed. Onyx sat down with me on his lap. I winced at the feel of his leather pants against my sore ass.

"You did so well. Are you alright? Was it too much?" He asked as his hand brushed my hair from my face.

"I ache," I answered honestly.

"What aches?" He asked.

I'm still shy about answering this question, even after what happened between us. Onyx waits patiently for my answer, and I know he expects me to answer.

"My pussy."

"Does your pussy need to be filled?" he chuckled. His finger slipped between my folds.

"Please," I moaned.

"Please, what? What do you need, sweet Rosa?" Onyx asked, his finger teased between my pussy lips.

"I need to cum." I breathed. He plunged two fingers inside

my pussy, and instantly, my vaginal walls clamped down around his digits. His thumb whisked my clit as his fingers fucked inside my cunt.

"Such a good girl." His deep voice vibrated through my body.

"Ah, so close." I moaned, and his fingers rapidly stroked my body.

"Cum, Rosa, cum for me." Onyx demands.

He pumped his fingers inside my channel, my orgasm quickly building. I lifted my hips from his lap, meeting his thrusts until, finally, I plummet over the edge. I cry out with my orgasm, and he kept stroking me through my peak.

"Such a greedy pussy, cumming for me. Fucking perfect." He hissed, then bit my neck and sucked. I screamed with another orgasm. Onyx removed his fingers from my body and brought them to my lips. "Suck." He ordered, pulling away from my neck briefly before he returned to feeding off of me. I immediately sucked his fingers into my mouth. My tongue slid over his fingers as I sucked them clean. He pulled his fangs from my neck and licked over the bite. Onyx removed his fingers from my mouth and kissed my cheek. I smiled at the gentle gesture.

"Intense?" He asked, his arms wrapped around my body. He pressed me tight against his broad bare chest. "I didn't mean to take your blood."

I nuzzled my cheek against him. I savored the feel of his muscular arms cocooning me against him. "I didn't expect it to feel like that," I whispered against his chest, my lips brushing his warm skin as I spoke.

"The spanking or the bite?" He asked.

"Both." I chuckled. "Is it crazy that I just let a stranger spank me, suck my blood, all the while giving me the most intense orgasms of my life?"

He lifted my chin with his thumb and forefinger and forced me to look up at him. "We are not exactly strangers."

"I guess not."

Onyx smiled. He weaved his fingers through my hair and dug into my scalp. He gave my hair a slight tug and forced my head back. His lips met mine as he leaned in. The kiss was light, timid, as if he was asking for permission. I opened my lips, and he slipped his tongue inside my mouth. He quickly deepened the kiss, and it's so powerful that if I was not sitting in his lap, my knees would buckle. We kissed until my lips felt swollen and bruised, but I didn't want it to end. I moaned into his mouth and wiggled in his lap. I wish I could feel his hard cock against my flaming ass cheeks without the barriers of his clothing.

Shyly, I slipped from his lap and went to my knees. I looked up at him, asking for permission. He knew what I wanted without speaking. He nodded and quickly undid his pants, freeing his cock.

It's so big and hard, I wasn't sure I could fit it in my mouth. He looked at me expectantly. I leaned in and took the base of his cock in my hand. I gathered my saliva in my mouth and licked along his length. Getting him nice and wet. My hand slid easily along his length. My eyes focused on the bead of pre-cum forming at his tip. I licked my lips before I lapped the bead from his cockhead.

"Yes, locked on mine." He demanded.

As I looked up at him, I swirled my tongue around his tip, concentrating on the underside. I slid my tongue along his length, licking and lightly sucking, before I moved back to the tip. I sucked his mushroomed shaped head into my mouth. His groans spurred me on.

I took him further into my mouth until his cock hit the back of my throat. His hands held both sides of my head and forced me to take him deeper. "Remove your hand." He snarled.

I did as he ordered and he took over, fucking my face, my throat. Forcing his cock down my throat, causing me to gag, but he liked me gagging. I felt him grow, stretching my throat. Tears and mascara ran down my cheeks. My mouth felt as if it was going to split open, but I wanted more. I wanted his cum. I wanted him to spray his cum all over my face. I didn't want to swallow it down my throat and not be able to taste it. I wanted to taste him, rub his essence into my skin.

His hips rose from the bed. I knew he was getting close. I tried to pull back, but he held me a moment longer before he yanked me off his cock. His hand went to his base and his load hit my face, hot and thick.

"Open your mouth." He panted.

I did and ate up as much cum as I could. His next wave shot on my tits, then he covered my face with the rest of his load. I cleaned him up, savoring every drop of cum. After his cock was clean, I lean back and rub his cum over my body. Goddess, I never knew I was such a cum slut.

He smirked at me and helped me from the floor and cradled me in his lap.

"Are you alright?" He asked.

I laughed. "Yes."

He gathered me in his arms and carried me to an adjoining bathroom. Onyx sat me on the vanity and ran the water in the sink. From a shelf, he grabbed a washcloth and wet it. He gently washed my face and down my body. He cleaned me up and then carried me back to bed.

"Get some rest, little human." He said once he stripped completely and slipped into bed with me.

CHAPTER 7

ROSA

I'm not sure how long I had been sleeping, but when I woke, I saw Onyx getting dressed.

"Onyx?" I whispered.

He looked over his shoulder at me. "I'm sorry, Rosa, but I have to go. They found the demon that attacked you."

I sat up and pulled the sheet to my chin. "I should go anyway."

"You can stay here. You'll be safe." He promised.

I shook my head. "I need to get home." Searching the room, I looked for my clothes. Once I spotted them, I stood with the sheet and snatched my dress up. I rushed into the bathroom.

"Rosa, I want to see you again." He said through the closed bathroom door.

"You don't have to say that. This was just sex." I said, zipping up the back of my dress.

Onyx burst through the door and was on me in seconds. His mouth slammed onto mine and forced his tongue inside my mouth. He devoured me, his fingers bit into my welted ass. And when he finally pulled away, we both were breathless.

"First, I don't say things I don't mean. Second, we didn't have sex. You gave me the best blow job of my life and I might have given you a few orgasms. But my sweet little human, when we have sex for the first time, you will not leave my bed for days." He snarled. "And third, you might not be ready for this part, but here it is. You are mine. You are my mate." His eyes softened, and he cupped my cheek. "Finish getting dressed. I'll take you home."

"Ummm, okay."

I had no idea what to say to him and honestly; I wasn't sure I wanted to correct anything he just said.

CHAPTER 8

ROSA

*T*rue to Onyx's word, the next time we had sex, I did not leave his bed for days. He took me from every imaginable position. I was on my hands and knees while he rammed me from behind. My head pressed against the mattress and my ass left for his pleasure. He speared inside my pussy so deep I felt him in my womb.

If not for his stronghold on my body while he fucked me, I think I might have been tossed from the bed with the force of Onyx fucking me. I craved the taste of his cum when he fucked my mouth. I longed for the taste of his blood that bound us together.

"You're finally home." I said and ran into his arms.

He didn't speak. He had me pinned against the wall in seconds. His lips were on mine and heat flowed through my body. He drew me into his demanding kiss. Onyx's desire was evident as he devoured my mouth. One of his hands gripped my hip, and the other found its way to my throat. He led our kiss with savage hunger.

He picked me up and my legs wrapped around his waist as he carried me to our bedroom. He smelled so good. Sandalwood and cedar. He pulled away from my lips. I could only describe the look in his eyes as savage desire. The fire burning there made his amber eyes glow. My stomach filled with butterflies and my legs trembled.

He lowered my body until my feet hit the floor. Then he yanked my head back by my hair and bit my neck. He ignored my moans as he sucked my essence into his mouth. When he finally pulled away, he hissed.

"Strip." He demanded as he pulled the zipper on my dress down my back.

I watched him step back and slowly undo his black dress shirt as I dragged my dress over my thighs and my hips. Revealing my black lace panties. He tossed his shirt to the chair. I yanked my dress up over my head and tossed it next to his clothes on the chair. Next, I undid my bra and tossed it.

"Fuck, Rosa." He growled, his eyes roaming over my body. His hand went to my panties and ripped them off of me in one hard pull.

My hands went to his belt. I fumbled with his belt. "What are you doing, gorgeous?"

"I've missed your taste." I whispered.

He chuckled. "I'm in charge. You will follow instructions and just enjoy. Free your mind. I want you to get out of your head and trust me."

Onyx bent his head and pressed his lips to mine. He brushed his over mine gently before moving down my cheek, my jaw, and to the curve of my neck. His hands cupped my breasts, he massaged them. I couldn't stop the whimpered moan that slipped through my lips.

"Do you trust me?" He asked.

"Yes." I breathed. I whispered. "Please."

"Such a good girl, begging." He praised. He picked me up

and dropped me in the center of the bed. He pulled his belt from his pants.

"Arms above your head." The command in his voice left little room for defiance. As soon as my arms were raised, he wrapped his belt around my wrists.

I squirmed on the bed, excitement and nerves fighting for dominance. He licked his lips, his eyes moving over my naked body. I watched him strip out of the rest of his clothes. His gigantic cock, thick and angry, made my mouth water.

"I need you," I begged.

"How bad do you need me?" He teased as he climbed between my legs. His length brushed my slit. I was drenched.

"So bad. I need you inside of me. Please," I begged.

"Good girl," he said as he pushed inside of my slick folds. I moaned as he pushed inside of me. "This first time is going to be fast and hard. I've missed you too much." He warned.

He quickly moved from slow thoughtful thrusts to pumping with unabandoned force. In and out of my pussy, he hit every nerve, every pleasure point over and over again.

His cock coaxed a waterfall of pleasure to flow out of me as he fucked me faster and faster. I wanted to scream my release.

"I want to hear you, Rosa." He hissed. "Let everything go."

His hand went to my throat and his hips pumped harder. His power over my body was surprising. I clenched around his cock as my orgasm tore through me. I screamed, and he continued to pound into me. He was getting close. I felt the tension in his body. He slammed back into me one last hard time. His head fell back on his shoulders, and he roared as his cum sprayed inside of me. I swear I saw stars as he filled me.

We stared at each other for a few moments before he collapsed beside me. I brought my arms down and allowed him to untie my wrists.

"I love you Rosa." He said as he pulled my body against his and buried his nose in the curve of neck.

"I love you, Onyx." I whispered.

"You're pregnant." He said.

"I know." I said with a smile.

"You're not shocked?" He asked, turning me to look at him.

"Not much has shocked me since moving to Hemlock Valley. After two months, I have a one-night stand with a sexy vampire who saved me from a demon. Then a day later, I am taken by said vampire and told that I am his mate. Not much surprises me." I said, then kissed his nose.

"The babe will be a vampire." He said, as if it was a warning.

"I figured she would be." I smiled.

"She?" He arched a brow.

"Of course, she."

"I can't have a girl. You must be wrong." He said. His face grew pale, and that was saying something. He was a vampire.

"Afraid she might be taken by a vampire, too?"

"Oh, gods." He grumbled and fell back against the mattress.

THE END FOR NOW

HEMLOCK VALLEY

SNEAKING AROUND WITH A TIGER

SKYLAR QUINN

CHAPTER 1

HEMLOCK INN – CHIP TAYLOR CIRCA 2012

"*C*hip Taylor, you get back here right now!"

I heard my mom yelling at me from across the house, but I knew better than to let her catch me. She was pissed that my girlfriend's mother just called and told her that she had caught Jenna and me in her bedroom, naked. It was Senior Year; we were adults. What did it matter? But our moms thought otherwise.

"I'll see you later, Mom!" I yelled back to her.

I heard the cuss words flying from her mouth as I ran out of the house and down the street. It was great being a young shifter. I had all the skills of an animal, but some human common sense. Literally, what more could I want?

Jenna and I promised to meet up after we dealt with our mothers at our secret rendezvous spot, and that was where I was going. This town had secrets, and I hadn't told her about mine. We had just lost our virginity to one another two days ago, so tonight would be the perfect night for me to share the fact that I was a tiger.

My parents told me this was a secret we kept and told no one until we were sure they were trustworthy. The only person I had trusted was Robert, my best friend. He was a human, but thought it was great that I had the ability to shift. It was time that I started branching out on my own and making my own choices.

I could feel my cell phone vibrating in my pants. I hoped it was Jenna. I pulled my phone out, looked at the screen and knew my wish was not granted. Reluctantly, I answered.

"Hey Dad."

"What the hell is wrong with you?" His anger was seeping through the phone.

"Nothing's wrong with me. Mom's the issue."

"Your mother isn't the issue. She told me Susan called. You and Jenna slept together."

I sighed. Why was this an issue? "Yes, we're 18, seniors. We both are graduating with honors. What's the deal?"

"You think you're a man and know everything, but you don't. There is still so much you don't know about being a shifter. And there are rules!"

"Dad," I said. "I'm a man. It's time I make my own choices."

"Just because you're legally a man doesn't mean you know anything about what will change now."

I rolled my eyes. "You sound like Mom. Seriously, Dad, let Jenna and I have our fun."

"Promise me you won't sleep with her again."

"No, I can't promise you that." I was getting angry now. Why were they being so unreasonable?

"You need to come home so we can talk to you about the ramifications when you, a shifter, sleep with someone."

"If I come home, will Mom cool her jets?"

My father sighed. "I will talk to your mom. Just come home."

I hung up the phone, not giving my dad an answer. I

started walking towards Jenna and our secret spot when his comment about me sleeping with someone as a shifter hit me. What did being a tiger shifter have to do with anything at all about sex? I wasn't fooling around with her as a tiger. At the end of the day, I didn't like being angry with my parents, and I didn't when my parents were mad at me either. So, I turned around and started walking back to my house.

~

JENNA ROOSEVELT'S HOUSE

"JENNA, NO, YOU CANNOT sleep around with that boy!" Her mom paced the room.

"Stop it, Mom." I started pacing the room, too. "You can't stop me. I'm eighteen! I've been an adult for months now!"

"It isn't about you being too young, it's about you being a witch!"

"Oh, my God! THIS AGAIN!" I yelled.

"Yes, this! Your grandmother was killed because she was a witch. You do not know what it is like for people to hunt you down."

"And you really think Chip is going to hunt me down and kill me?"

"Jenna, I should have told you more about our family. This is my fault. My mother was killed."

"Stop, I know! A serial killer killed Grammy. That has nothing to do with me."

"Jenna, sit. Let me talk."

I threw my hands in the air and knew nothing would change if I didn't let her talk. I walked to my bed, sat down, brought my knees to my chest, wrapped my arms around myself, and said, "Okay, talk."

Mom walked to my desk, pulled my chair out, and

brought it over to the bed. "Jenna, sweetie, Grandma was killed by a mystical creature who couldn't control their rage."

"What kind of mystical creature? Like us, a witch?"

"You know how this town is made up of different creatures?"

"Yeah, but we don't talk about it. Like the worst-kept secret. Kind of like Salem."

Mom nodded. "Right. The town knows the secrets, but everyone else doesn't. They only suspect. But our family has always kept quiet."

I nodded. "Yeah, I know, it makes no sense. Like, why can't I talk to anyone about being a witch?"

"What I never told you about Grammy is that the creature was a shifter who hated witches. She was killed because this wolf hated our kind."

"That's horrible, but I don't understand what that has to do with me and Chip."

My mother lowered her head and reached for my hand. "Honey, he's a shifter."

I shrugged my shoulders, "Okay, so? He didn't kill Grammy."

"But his kind did. There is a reason your father and I haven't set foot in the Inn or Cherry's Café."

"That sounds an awful lot like prejudice. You can't blame an entire species for one person's evil."

Mom stood up and started pacing again. "Jenna, no, don't start with me on that."

I shook my head, "No, Mom. No. I love Chip and me and him are serious. You either get on board or I'll leave once I am done with high school."

"You wouldn't leave." Mom crossed her arms across her chest. The anger on her face was evident.

"Why did you let me date him this whole time anyway if you hated his kind?"

"We thought it was casual. If I had known you were going

to drop your pants for him, I would have stopped you right at the start."

"I didn't just drop my pants." I stood up, walked across the room, grabbed my purse, and turned to her. "I'm leaving. I'll be back later."

"Jenna, stop, you will not meet that boy!"

"Yes, Mom, I am. I'm eighteen, you can't stop me."

CHAPTER 2

HEMLOCK INN – CHIP TAYLOR

There was no way I wanted to walk into my house right now, but here I was, doing what my parents wanted me to do. As the front door pushed open, I heard my mom talking from the kitchen.

"I should have told him from the start when he started dating her."

"You can't beat yourself up Julie, we both didn't think it would get this serious."

My mom was crying, I could tell. "Jeff, what if they mate?"

"Then we have a daughter-in-law."

"Their children may not be one of us, though."

I heard my dad laugh. "Seriously, is that what you're hung up on? That she is human?"

"Don't laugh. This is important. There aren't many tigers left in this part of the world. He needs to do what we did and marry another tiger shifter. We grew to love each other."

"Julie, we don't even know how many times they have had sex. They could have already mated."

Mated? What were they talking about? This seemed like a good time to walk into the room and talk with them. "Mom, Dad, why are you two talking about mating?"

Both of them turned around and looked at me. My mom's eyes were puffy from crying. "Chip, you came back!" She got up from the table and rushed to me, wrapping her arms around me. "Please sit down."

"Yeah, we have a lot of things to discuss," my dad said.

I walked across the room and sat at the other side of the table, so I could look at both of them at the same time. "Okay, I'm here, talk. Start with the mating stuff I heard."

"Chip, you know that sex as shifters is different, right?" My mom started with.

"Julie, let me do this." My dad looked at me and shrugged. "It isn't really different. It's just complicated."

"What do you mean different, Mom?"

"Like your dad said, it's complicated. How many times have you and Jenna had sex?"

I didn't want to talk about this with my parents, not at all. "Twice the other night."

"Twice, eh," my dad chuckled.

"Jeff don't encourage it. You know what could happen."

"Well, it was more like one and a half. I didn't finish the second time. Why does this matter?"

"Because, Son," my dad said. "If you have sex with the same person over and over, it increases the likelihood of mating."

"You keep saying mating, do you mean getting married? Her and I have already talked about that, if it makes you freak out more."

"Married! You're eighteen!" My mom hollered.

"Focus Julie. No, Chip, mating is far more serious than marriage. Mating is for life, and you can't undo it."

"So, tell me what it is then if it is so serious."

"You know the matching tattoos your mother and I have?"

I nodded. "Yes, your weird symbols."

Mom smiled. "We got that the third time we had sex. It was so painful and romantic all at once."

"Huh?"

"When you mate, your souls connect and become one. A symbol that is unique to each couple will appear."

"Like in the movies? No fucking way." I couldn't believe they thought I would fall for this.

"Yes, you can say it's like the movies. It means we can only procreate with each other. No one else could bear a child from either of us. At least not until one of us dies." My dad grabbed my mom's hand. "But we don't want that to happen anytime soon, do we, Julie?"

Mom shook her head. "No, we don't." Then she looked at me. "You have to stop having sex with her. Or else you risk becoming mated. You two are not old enough to know you want to be in this for life. Because that's what it would be, life."

"This isn't your call to make. But what were you two talking about, if we had kids?"

"That's the other thing, Son," Dad said. "We have no way of knowing, if you have a child with Jenna, if it would be a shifter or a human."

"What does that matter? It isn't my job to repopulate the tiger community."

"It's all of our jobs," Mom said.

"Then why did you only have one kid?" I shot back in a snarky tone.

"That's not fair to say to your mother. You know what she went through."

I knew she lost a baby and lost her female parts in the process. Mom cried for days afterward.

"Sorry, Mom, I didn't mean to be an asshole. I'm just

mad." Our eyes locked, and I knew my mother loved me more than anything. "Really, I'm sorry."

"It's okay. Just please, Chip, you gotta think twice."

"Look, I appreciate what you're doing. But this is Jenna and my decision. We love each other and have been talking about this for a while. Well, sex and marriage, that is. I'm going to tell her I'm a shifter, too. And you can't stop me."

I could tell they both wanted to say something but held back their words. That was probably smart because I was angry about all of this lecture and didn't want to take any more grief.

"We love you; you know that right?" Dad said to me as if all of this was the end. It was so final sounding.

"Yes Dad, and I love you both too. But I also love Jenna. So, whatever will be, will be."

Mom stood up from the table and looked down at me and then at my dad. She wanted to keep talking but instead turned around and went upstairs.

"Is Mom ever going to forgive me?"

Dad smiled. "She will when you have your first child."

"Hell, I don't want her to be mad at me for a decade." Both Dad and I laughed. "But I'm going to go now. I don't know when I will be home."

Dad nodded his head. "Be safe. I will talk to you in the morning."

I left the house again for the second time and went straight to Jenna and my secret place. I ran along the lake, trying to avoid anyone seeing me. I wanted no more distractions. All I wanted was her. And to tell her my secret.

When I saw our special tree in the distance, I noticed that under it was a blanket spread out, and my Jenna. Jenna beat me here. My heart raced seeing her. I knew there was one important thing I had to do before we continued this night.

CHAPTER 3

HEMLOCK VALLEY LAKE – JENNA ROOSEVELT

I sat there under the tree, gazing off into the distance. My heart hurt at the idea of not being able to be with Chip. So much of our time together was spent dreaming of our future and the lives we would lead. But one thing was evident, we both still had secrets we hadn't shared. Did that mean we had trust issues? Or maybe that meant we were still putting our family first, not our relationship?

At eighteen, did stuff like this even matter? I wasn't even sure which of the things my mother lectured me on I needed to dwell on first. What I needed was Chip. I would deal with the consequences of my mother later. Right now, it was about my needs. There were eight weeks left in the school year and after that, I would have a diploma and could figure out how to make it on my own. The days of parental control and dictation would be over.

My phone buzzed, and I saw my mom's name pop up on the screen. I didn't want to answer it. The school guidance counselor told me once that if the person didn't make me happy, it was okay to cut them off. Maybe that applied to unreasonable parents too. I pressed the ignore button on my iPhone and put it back in my pocket.

A phone, that was one thing I would have to be responsible for on my own, just like food, shelter, and a car. Maybe I could survive walking and using the bus system.

There was a chill from the wind swirling around me, and my body shivered. I had brought a little picnic bag full of stuff. The blanket I was sitting on, some sandwiches I had made earlier, along with some water, fruit, and crackers. But I was glad I remembered to grab a sweater too.

I was pulling the sweater down over my head when I saw him. I could see his smile from across the grassy way. With a speed reserved only for emergencies, I shot up from the ground and ran towards him. There was nothing else in this world I wanted more than to kiss him. It was seeing him run towards me that pushed the whole moment over the top.

"Jenna," he said as he wrapped his arms around me.

"I love you," came out right before his lips planted on my mouth.

There was no such thing as being too young. What we felt was powerful and meaningful.

"I love you too," he said in between kisses.

Somehow, we made it back to the blanket, and he lowered me onto it.

"Jenna, I need to talk to you."

Nodding my head, "I do too. But first, just make love to me."

There was a look of hesitation in his eyes that was there for a few seconds. I almost thought he was going to say no, but then he kissed me again. Our bodies rolled around on the sheet, our hands exploring each other's bodies.

"Sit up," he ordered.

Wondering what made him talk in such a commanding tone, I sat up and tilted my head at him.

"You want to make love, fine. I want to have you completely submit to me."

Oh, he wanted to be kinky. That was great! Nodding my head, "I want to be yours."

"Good. Take your shirt off."

Chills ran up my spine at hearing his words. I reached down and pulled up the sweater and shirt I had on. My breasts bounced out of the clothing as I sat there before him in my bra and jeans.

"Bra too," he said.

Easily disposing of the bra, I grinned at him.

"You're such an obedient woman. I should have done this the first night."

I smiled at him, making sure he saw my enjoyment. When he reached out and ran his fingers over my breasts, it was like all of my nerve endings were on fire. I moaned out in pleasure when his fingers took my nipples between them and rolled them, playing and teasing my body.

"You still have pants on, my sexy woman."

I wasn't an honor student by luck, I was smart. I knew what he wanted. Jumping up, I kicked my shoes off, unbuttoned my pants, and pulled both jeans and panties to the ground. After stepping out of them, I sat back down on the blanket, smiling at this person I loved.

"Perfection," was the last thing he said before leaning over and putting his mouth around my breast. He was like a vacuum, the way he sucked at my nipple. His hand pushed my legs apart and then dove into my nether region. I was hot and wanting. He was delivering me my pleasure.

His fingers wiggled around inside of me, thrusting in and out. He teased my walls, my g-spot, and my clit all in a systematic rhythm. It was as if he knew which part of my body was in the most need.

"Chip, oh, Chip!" I cried out as he made my body feel

things I had never felt before. It was like he was imprinting on my aura somehow.

"Yes, Jenna, let go," he said.

My body was twisting and turning as his fingers teased me. I closed my eyes and tried to clear my mind of everything to just be in this moment. When he slid his cock in me, I felt something magical happen. It was an out-of-this-world sensation. I had read in an old grimoire that sex enhanced magic. Maybe that was happening now, and I didn't realize I was using my powers.

"Holy shit, Jenna, you're like a furnace; so hot deep inside."

His words made me want more. I wrapped my legs around him and pushed my hips up, deepening his thrusts. It was the purest feeling I could have imagined.

When our eyes locked, I noticed he started to make his special face. I knew he was about to let it all go. I didn't care that we weren't using a condom. I wanted it. I wanted all of him inside of me.

"Oh, my God," Chip cried out as his release overtook him. His cock felt like it was growing inside of me and suddenly my mom's comment about him being a shifter became important.

"Chip," I moaned as we both released our orgasms.

"Jenna," he mirrored.

When our bodies stopped, the cool breeze was gone, and it felt like we were on fire. His skin was hot to the touch, and I felt like I had a fever.

Then, almost in unison, both of us started screaming.

"Aaaahhhhh," I bellowed out.

My eyes shot down to my left wrist. I turned my arm over and watched as my skin started searing in a design I had never seen before.

Had I done this? Had I used magic to give myself a tattoo?

But then I realized Chip was screaming too. I looked up

at him and he was grabbing his left arm, and he had the same emblem burned into his flesh.

Oh fuck! What have I done?

"Chip, we have to talk!"

He started shaking his head. "Jenna, I'm so sorry. I never gave you the option."

Our eyes locked, and I started to cry. *What had we just done?*

CHAPTER 4

HEMLOCK VALLEY – CHIP TAYLOR - CIRCA 2025

*I*t was hard coming home each year to see my folks when Jenna's mother wanted nothing to do with us. It was our daughter's twelfth birthday, and my parents had planned a huge celebration. They even rented out the gazebo. But it never failed, somehow each visit we had in the last decade ended with Jenna and her mother Susan fighting over our daughter Sunshine.

"Dad, will Paw-Paw and Grandma take me to the movies for my birthday, like they do every year?"

I looked at my little girl in the back seat through the rearview mirror. We would know soon if she got my gene or not. This was the birthday that would change it all.

"You know you're getting a different party this year. It's your special one, the big one-two!"

Jenna looked over at me and smiled. "Miracles are known to happen every twelve years or so."

I reached out to my wife and squeezed her hand. "Yes, they are."

"What about your parents, Momma? Will they come?"

It broke our hearts that Jenna's family had never accepted that she mated and married a shifter. My family quickly got over any anger, once they knew we intended to honor the mating. Now my mother is like Jenna's second mom. We're all happy together and our pack accepted Jenna as part of the in-law club. That's what we called the people who married into the pack but weren't shifters.

Seeing the reminders of Jenna's family every day was too much. After Sunshine was born, we packed up and moved to Salem. I thought it was time Jenna learned to be proud of being a witch, and there wasn't anywhere else that could offer her the rich history.

"Today's going to be a great party, kiddo. All the family will be here, that you know and love. Just enjoy this weekend, okay?"

Sunshine had been a preemie. Born six weeks early. I always wondered if it was because she had a shifter inside her and that meant she developed faster; that was just my theory. Tomorrow night was the full moon, the first one after she turned twelve. Either her body would start to change, or it wouldn't. The first change always happened at the full moon, and then after that, we all learned to control the change.

It was hard for me at first, my emotions always made my fingernails shoot out of my hands. At thirteen, it became a real issue when I started shifting every time I got horny. But luckily, I got it under control, fast. My dad was a tremendous help in that sense. Hopefully, my mom could help Sunshine like that too.

Jenna was worried while she was breastfeeding that Sunshine would shift into a tiger cub and try to eat her breast. We used to joke about it way too much.

We had a great life, and I knew tonight would be perfect for our little girl.

"Do you feel any different?" Jenna asked.

Sunshine laughed, "Mom, you keep asking me that? I told you I'm fine. What, do you expect me to start getting my period now that I'm twelve?"

"Something like that," Jenna said, chuckling.

"I'm not ready for that level of anger in the house monthly. Her period could stay away for a long time," I teased.

"Daddy!" Sunshine scolded.

"Yeah, Dad, stop being mean to our baby."

I saw my parents' car parked across from the gazebo on South Pedal Lane. I pulled the car into the parking space next to it and turned around, looking at my daughter in the back seat. "I just want you to stay my baby girl forever. I won't be sorry for that."

Jenna's hand touched my arm, and we smiled at each other.

"I love both my girls. Now Sunshine, go find your grandparents. It's time for you to turn twelve!"

We watched Sunshine run away from the car and into the park where my parents were setting things up for her.

"Mom told me she sent an invitation to your house, and she saw your mom at the store and spoke to her."

Jenna looked at me with hope in her eyes, "I told you; miracles could happen."

"Just don't get your hopes up."

We got out of the car and walked over to where the party was.

≈

JENNA TAYLOR

EVERY YEAR WE CELEBRATE Sunshine's birthday here. A tradition that we started when she was one. This year, it was very different for me. I had never cared if Sunshine ended up a shifter or a witch. It wasn't that. It was that this was such a huge day for my daughter, and my parents would probably not show up.

Over the years, my father sent me money and snuck phone calls or text messages. But he hadn't seen his grand-child since she was nine months old. I blamed my mom for that. But the reality was, he was a grown man who could make his own choices if he wanted to.

Mr. and Mrs. Taylor took me into their family, loved me and my daughter. It was great to have them in our lives. But I missed my own family. And now, if Sunshine doesn't have any shifter blood, she would need the help my parents could give her, from our ancestral strength. Mom never passed it down to me after, I showed up with the mating mark on my arm.

At first, she thought we went out and got matching tattoos. I never should have corrected her. But when we decided to get married, I told her the truth. And that was the end of it. I had betrayed her, and all my aunts and uncles.

"It's going to be okay, Jenna. I promise."

"I hope so, Chip."

"Come on, sweetheart, let's go celebrate our daughter."

We got out of the car and Chip went to the trunk to grab Sunshine's presents. We walked together across the park and placed our stuff on the gift table. My mother-in-law had done a wonderful job with the decorations. Sunshine looked on top of the world, playing with the other kids from the pack who had already arrived.

"I don't want to alarm you, but I spoke to your mother." Julie's voice scared me. She appeared out of nowhere, always so silent and stealth-like.

"Thank you for trying."

"Of course, sweetheart. You're our family and so is that little girl. Today is going to be a big day. I can sense it."

"She says she doesn't feel any different," I shared with my mother-in-law.

"She won't feel it until tomorrow when the moon starts to rise."

Chip walked over to his mother and hugged her. "That's why we came home, to be with you, Mom,"

"And we are so glad that you did." Julie hugged me too and we all sat back and watched the young girl of the hour with infectious laughter. We all knew that tomorrow could be life changing.

CHAPTER 5

JENNA TAYLOR ~ HEMLOCK INN

"*Y*our parents made Sunshine feel special today," I said to Chip, who was undressing.

"They did. It was great seeing everyone from the pack show up and support her."

Chip and I locked eyes. He knew what I was thinking without me saying a word. "I'm sorry they didn't show up."

I nodded at my husband, "Me too. We leave on Sunday, so there is always a possibility they could show up."

"Yes, there always is." Chip walked around the bed and grabbed my hand. "But I know it isn't easy for you. It will be okay, I promise." His head lowered as he brought my hand to his mouth and kissed my palm.

"Don't make promises you can't keep." I tried to keep my voice steady, but I was far from okay. I just wanted a reconnection and reconciliation. Not just for me, but for Sunshine, too.

"Honey, you leave it all to me. Now," he paused and kissed my hand again, "why don't you let me help you forget your troubles, at least for a night?" Chip gave me the most wicked grin.

"I can get on board with that," I smirked. My insides were already swimming, thinking of what Chip had in mind.

His hands moved to grab the hem of my shirt and pulled the material up, stripping my torso of the garment. The chill in the room gave my skin goosebumps. The gleam in his eye made my lower region tingle.

"Chip," I said in a breathy voice.

"Jenna," he responded, before crushing his lips against mine.

The actions from that moment on were a blur as he finished stripping my clothes from our bodies and tossing me into bed. It didn't matter that we were in an inn. He was all animal, and my body craved this kind of attention. My back was pressed against the mattress, and I looked into my husband's eyes. The thing I loved most about these tender moments was what his eyes did. I wasn't sure if this was the normal shifter experience, but when Chip was horny and wanted me, his pupils glowed. A golden halo encircled his normal dark brown eyes, and I just knew that look was for me and only for me.

I heard him growl right before he pounced on me. Our bodies smashed together as he captured my mouth and stole kiss after kiss from me. His hand traveled down my body and found my core. His fingers slipped inside, and he started playing with my sensitive bud with his thumb. He had learned over the years the quickest ways to make my body respond to his touch. The benefit of being married is years of practice.

"Oh, Chip," my lips opened, and I moaned out, over and over as he worked my pussy over with his fingers. "Chip! I need you in me." I was panting, trying to hold my composure and save that release for his dick. "I need your cock in me!"

"Yes, ma'am," he growled, and as quickly as he had dove

inside me with his fingers, his cock was now slipping across my warm lips.

Chip brought his three fingers to my mouth; his grin told me he wanted to be dirty tonight. I opened and as he slipped his fingers into my mouth, my tongue cleaned each of his digits. I ran the muscle along each of his fingers, making sure to not waste a drop of my juice.

He pumped his cock over and over. My legs moved to wrap around his hips. I pushed up on my back, meeting his hips with my own, applying more force for friction. His cock pounded into the back of my pussy, as if his cockhead would slip through and into my womb.

"Oh, God!" I moaned out.

"No, wait!" Chip said. He pulled his body away from me, his cock slipping out of my cunt.

"What?" I asked, but he silenced me with one action. He put his hands on my hips, picked me up, and then turned me over onto all fours. His hands held onto my hips, and then I felt his cock slip inside me once again.

Doggie style. He loved doing it doggie.

His hand went to my hair. I felt his fingers massaging my scalp before grabbing a fist full of hair and pulling right around it. My head and chest arched up, following his command, and then I felt him shoving himself deeper inside me over and over.

The magic in my body swirled around me. When we moved to Salem, I learned that my magic could be enhanced by sex. It was a powerful tool when used with someone you truly loved, and I loved Chip.

"Yes, yes!" I panted out in praise of him using my body. I knew what was about to happen, and when my orgasm rushed through my body, my magical powers coursed through my pores sending out a beacon to anyone paying attention.

"Fuck," Chip groaned out as I felt his cock enlarge. The

head of his penis filled my pussy completely. When Chip knotted, I knew we would be stuck together for a few extra minutes. Our bodies were locked as one as Chip's load poured into me.

In my mind, I could visualize his sperm swimming through my canal and implanting inside me. That experience had only happened one other time... the night Sunshine was conceived.

My world was being rocked in an amazing way when I heard the knock at the door. My name was called, and I recognized that voice.

"Jenna, I need to talk to you."

I whipped my head around and looked Chip in his eyes. He could see my panic, and we looked at the bedroom door. Maybe we had imagined it.

But then the knock happened again. "Jenna, I heard you two. I'll be downstairs when you're ready."

My mother had just interrupted what may have been another child being conceived. I didn't know what to do, so I stayed frozen.

"Baby, you have to go down and talk to her."

I felt his cock shrinking and then it slipped out of my pussy.

"Yeah, I know."

"I'll help you get cleaned up and dressed. We will go see her together."

～

Ten minutes later, Chip and I were walking down the stairs. When we stepped into the foyer, we noticed my mother sitting on the couch in the main living area. She was talking with Julie, and they had cups of coffee in front of them. My dad was sitting next to my mom. I couldn't believe it. Sunshine sat next to Chip's mom, smiling and happy that her grandparents had actually shown up.

"Jenna," my mom said, as she stood up and smiled at me.

"Hi Mom, Dad," I said, looking at both of them.

"Chip, why don't you and I take Sunshine into the kitchen for a late-night treat? It is her birthday, after all." Julie was always so polite.

He nodded, "Come on kiddo, I know where my mom hides the good cookies."

"Score!" Sunshine jumped up yelling, as she raced out of the room with my husband and mother-in-law.

When everyone had cleared, I looked at my parents, walked across the room, and sat down where Julie had been seated. "Glad you could make the time for Sunshine's birthday," was the first thing I could think of to say.

"I'm sorry," my mother said. "We should have come earlier. And I don't just mean today."

"Jenna, we should have come every year," my dad chimed in.

"But you didn't." I sat with my shoulders back, my spine straight as an arrow, and with an unwavering bravado in my voice.

"And that's my fault, Jenna. I was severely selfish, to you, your dad, and worse, Sunshine."

"You were. What made you change your mind now?" My eyes darted back and forth between my parents.

"Julie," Dad finally said after some moments of silence. "She wouldn't let it go and forced your mom to face her fears. Julie came over tonight and talked with us."

God bless that woman, I thought to myself.

"Jenna, I want, no, we want to be in your lives. We have so many years to make up for."

"Julie also explained to us the significance of this birthday and what will be discovered tomorrow. I convinced your mother that, shifter or not, our granddaughter needs to know her heritage."

"Not just your granddaughter. I do too. You stopped teaching me everything when we mated."

I was pointing my words at my mother because I knew she had made those choices.

"Yes, you need it too. I'm sorry Jenna, I am. I let my hate and anger get the best of me and now we have lost so much time. What can I do to show you that I'm sorry?"

Shrugging my shoulders, "I don't know. But for now, having cookies with us is a start." I stood up and walked toward the foyer again but stopped and turned around. "But never interrupt Chip and me making love again."

I walked off toward the kitchen when I heard my father say to my mother, "You didn't tell me that's what was going on!"

That made me smile. I wasn't sure why, but it did.

CHAPTER 6

CHIP TAYLOR - HEMLOCK VALLEY LAKE

I sat on the back porch of the Inn watching the sun start to set. We were gathered around, waiting on our Sunshine to see which path she would take. It was a weird sensation being a parent; knowing that our actions would absolutely affect others around us. But there was no greater love than holding your child in your arms when they were born. Now I had to hope and pray that my baby girl would join the pack tonight.

My first time shifting was scary. While this town had always been open to the magical elements, I was taught to hide it. I don't want to be like that with Sunshine. I want her to embrace her path.

"You look deep in thought," my dad said as he sat beside me.

"Today's an important day. It changes everything."

He nodded and handed me a glass of scotch. "I remember when you changed. Of course, we didn't have the same antic-ipation that is going on right now, but I was scared. Scared you would get tied up in the high we all have when we run free in our animal form."

"I do love being a tiger. I think that's why I want Sunshine to be one so much. That instant connection."

"Son, she has that connection with you, regardless of how tonight ends."

"I know. But maybe I'm being selfish for wanting more than I have."

"It is being selfish. Now, come on, let's go stand by her and help her through this, one way or another."

We walked down the stairs and over to the backyard that faced the grocery store. "How are you doing, kiddo?" I grabbed my daughter's hand and pulled her in for a hug.

"Nervous," she said.

"Nothing to be nervous about. You're going to be a ferocious tiger or an amazing witch. Either way, you're a badass in my book."

"Your dad's right. Either way, you're amazing."

"When does this happen?" my mother-in-law asked. I didn't love that she was here as if she had been accepting of this family all along. But I would not kick her out. My wife and daughter needed them in their lives.

"It should be any minute now if it is going to happen," my mother pointed out.

"Mom, Dad," Sunshine said.

We all looked down at her and I could see tears starting to form. "Sweetie, what's wrong?"

"I don't feel anything. I wanted to be able to run in the forest with you!"

"Oh, honey," I said, dropping to my knees. "We can run in the forest and be free without you shifting."

The sun was almost completely set, and the moon was up. We all knew what was happening.... A new witch was being born.

"I'll help you with your powers," Jenna said as she knelt beside us.

"No, we all will," Susan said, walking behind Sunshine and placing a hand on her shoulders. "I'll show you and your mother the old ways."

"I'm sorry, Dad." Sunshine looked into my eyes.

I pulled her in for a hug. "Nothing to be sorry for, kiddo. Come on, Grandma has a cake in the kitchen with your name on it."

As we all walked back to the porch of the Inn, Susan touched my arm, and I stopped. We locked eyes and something unexpected happened.

"I'm sorry Chip."

"I know you are."

She shook her head. "No, I'm sorry you didn't get what you wanted. Your tiger cub."

Now it was my turn to shake my head no. "It was never about her being what I wanted. It was always about her openly celebrating what she was. Witch or shifter didn't matter. It was always about her being accepted for her true nature."

"I know I made all of this so complicated for you and her over the last decade," my mother-in-law said.

"Really, longer than that. But I accept your apology, Susan."

As we walked back to the house, I got to thinking about the night Sunshine was made. There was so much we didn't know about, and now I was faced with the reality of our little girl growing up and meeting someone of her own. One day there would be a man who would take her away from us.

It was at that moment that I truly forgave my in-laws because I could finally put myself in their shoes.

"You're always deep in thought," Jenna said to me, as she poked the side of my ribs.

"What can I say? I'm a thinker."

"You're an eater, and this cake is calling your name."

～

JENNA TAYLOR

IT WAS A LONG day waiting in anticipation for Sunshine's journey to unfold, but now I was ready for my journey.

"You ready for bed?" Chip asked me.

"Not quite." I shot him a glance and smirked.

"Oh?" He walked over, grinning. "And what are you ready for then, Mrs. Taylor?"

"I'm ready for something a little more adult in nature." I leaned over and placed my lips on my husband's neck. I let my tongue tease his skin. I felt his body twitch under my touch.

"I'm listening," he said, as he put his hands under my shirt and lightly tickled my sides.

"You know, now that witches officially outnumber shifters in our house, things are going to change."

Chip barked out a laugh. "Oh, are they now?"

I nodded, "Yes. For starters, new rules will be implemented and if you can't follow them, there will be punishment of the witchy variety."

"For the record, you're making sexy talk out of the fact our daughter is the new witch."

I started to talk and then stopped. "Okay, way to ruin the moment, smartass."

Chip pulled me close to him and took my lips with his own. There was a fire that swirled around us as our souls meshed together. "There is always a moment when you and I are together. Nothing will ruin that."

"Good. I have something else to tell you." I pulled away from him and took his hand in mine.

"What do you have to tell me?"

"What would you say if I told you there was a way to balance the power back?"

Chip grinned, "There is only one way to do that, and if that was on the table, you would have already told me so." He grabbed my hips, lifted me in the air, and tossed me on the bed. "And I would have known if it was possible."

"Or maybe you were so seduced you missed the moment."

Chip looked at me in a confused manner. "Okay, I'm lost. What are you saying? Because for a moment, I thought you were saying we're pregnant again."

I laughed. I smiled at the man I loved and said, "We are."

There was pure joy in his eyes as he looked at me. "I can't believe we're going to have another one. How long have you known?"

I shrugged. "A couple of days. I didn't want to take anything away from Sunshine. Remember last month when we left Sunshine with the babysitter?"

Chip smirked, "This is the perfect ending to the day."

"It really is. I love you so much, Chip."

"I love you too, Jenna."

My body curled into his, and he held me close. "We're going to have to move, get a bigger place." I paused, thinking about the house we lived in. "Maybe we should move home."

"You would want to come back home? After everything?"

I nodded, "Yeah, because I miss my parents, and if they will bridge the gap and help me teach the art of witchcraft to Sunshine, then I would be a fool to say no."

Chip's hands danced along my skin, "If that's what you want, we can put our house on the market next week."

"Thank you," I said. "It is what I want."

"Do you want to know what I want?" He wiggled his eyebrows at me.

Laughter escaped, and I wiggled my way out of his grasp and mounted him. "I think I know what you want." My hands started unbuttoning his pants.

"You're so smart, I'm glad the pregnancy brain hasn't set in yet." He laughed at me as I swatted at him.

"Bad kitty," I scolded.

"Hey now, there is only one person who gets to do the punishing around here and that's me." Chip stood up while holding onto me. He spun us around and then plopped me down on the bed. "And speaking of kitty's, there is only one of those in this room and I'm about to devour it."

My body shivered as he talked about my pussy. "Yes, please."

"Good little witch," he laughed.

"Hey now, careful or I'll turn you into a mouse."

We were both laughing and teasing. Our love making had been different this time. It was tender and sweet.

After, we laid in each other's arms, enjoying the post-orgasm bliss.

"Another child is going to be a blessing," Chip said.

"He will."

"You can't be so sure it's a boy."

I smiled, "I know it's a boy; I can sense it."

"Well, selfishly I hope you're right."

Nodding my head, "Let's get some sleep. We can share the news with everyone tomorrow."

"Good idea. I love you, Jenna."

"I love you too, Chip."

he End.

HEMLOCK VALLEY

WEREWOLF TAKES A MATE

SUNNY A MORGAN

CHAPTER 1

KEYLA VOLKOV

I sighed as the sign for Hemlock Valley came into view. The end of my life as I knew it was about to be over. It was time for me to face my fate and the man I was forced to marry. Zev Lykoudis. Zev was the eldest son of the River Moon Pack's alpha. I was the eldest daughter of the Shadow Pack's alpha. Our packs have been on shaky terms for over fifty years. Recently, things have been getting dangerous for both packs. A union between the packs was needed.

My oldest brother, Raff, mated Alpha Lykoudis' daughter, Daciana, and they had a son. Both packs were happy about the union until Raff killed Daciana. My brother had been drugged by a group of scientists. They had kidnapped him and performed numerous experiments on Raff. When he was finally rescued, he wasn't himself. He was literally a wild animal. No one knows exactly what happened between Raff and Daciana. My nephew Billy had been spending the night with my father. When he brought Zev to my brother's home, he found my sister-in-law's body. Raff was a mess and had a gun in his hand. He shot himself in front of my nephew and my father.

Daciana's family hated us now. I couldn't blame them. Our pack didn't protect her. Now, to keep peace, another union needed to be made. Zev and I were that union. To my surprise, it was Zev who suggested our marriage. But it came with a price to Shadow's pack. Zev would be raised in River Moon's pack.

If I was honest, I was glad Zev would not be raised by my father. Alpha Volkov was a bastard. He would ruin Zev, just like he ruined my mother, my brother, and me.

I shook my head. To clear it from the dark thoughts. I needed to get to Hemlock Valley, marry Zev, and go get my nephew. My father kept Zev hostage until the marriage and treaty were completed.

Zev couldn't be as bad as my father, so really this wasn't a bad thing. Right? At least that's what I kept telling myself.

As I drove through the town square; I was surprised by how at ease I felt. What was it about this place that gave me an instant calming feeling? I was supposed to meet Zev at Cherrie's Cafe. He said I couldn't miss it and he was right. Main drag, corner location with a big sign with Cherrie's Cafe in flashing red and pink lights.

Once I found the cafe, I drove around the corner to a parking lot just off Dalia Street and walked two blocks to the cafe.

"Sit anywhere, sweetie." An elderly lady yelled from behind the counter. I nodded and found an empty booth by the window.

"My name is Deb. I'll be your server. Can I get you a drink while you look at the menu?" She asked.

"Yes, sweet tea. I'm meeting someone. He should be here any minute." I said as I opened the menu.

"I'll keep an eye out for your date." Deb said, as she skipped off.

ZEV LYKOUDIS

I CRACKED MY NECK BEFORE walking into Cherrie's. I recognized her immediately. If I had to saddle myself with a wife, at least she was gorgeous.

Keyla gave me a brief smile and a wave when she saw me at the front of the café. I nodded and walked the few feet to her booth.

"Hi, Keyla." I said as I slid into the booth sitting across from her.

"Hi Zev," she replied.

"Did you have any problems finding the place?" I asked.

"No, just where you said it was. Hard to miss."

"Good. Did you order?"

"Just sweet tea. I wasn't sure what your plans were." She said before taking a sip of her tea.

"My plans are to feed you, get you settled and plan this shame of a marriage." I sighed.

"Wow. You can't even pretend to be cordial." She snapped.

I leaned back in my sit. "Look, I'm sorry about how that came out. I just came off a week of double shifts and I'm exhausted. But we both know this isn't a love match."

She seemed to relax a bit and slumped back against the booth. "Just for the record, I wasn't looking to get tied down to you, either. But here we are. This was your idea, after all."

"It was this or bloodshed. This arrangement isn't about us, it's about what is best for the pack. What's best for our nephew." I said as I waved over Deb to take our order.

"Your usual Zev?" Deb asked.

"What else?" I winked at her.

"What about you, honey?" Deb asked Keyla.

"Bacon, cheeseburger, with everything but onions. Side of fries and a strawberry shake."

"Gotcha. Two bacon, cheeseburgers, loaded hold the onions, two sides of fries and two strawberry shakes. Two peas in a pod." Deb chuckled and walked off.

"Looks like we share the same appetites." Keyla said.

"Let's hope so." I muttered.

She raised her perfectly arched brow but didn't say anything.

CHAPTER 2

KEYLA VOLKOV

Zev Lykoudis was gorgeous. Nothing average about him. He was tall, broad, dark hair, and caramel colored eyes. I wanted to get lost in. Zev was the kind of man that gave you all kinds of thoughts. Wicked, dirty, and delicious thoughts. I should be happy he was so attractive, but instead it made me nervous. He was a means to an end. Zev was my nephew's only salvation from my father and I would do anything to make this work. Even if it came with a cost to my freedom. I tried not to fidget across from him, but everything about this man screamed, danger. He was dangerous because looking at him; I knew he was someone I could love. Love was a dangerous game between a Volkov and Lykoudis

"After we eat, I can take you to my house and get you settled." I said as Deb dropped off our food.

"I'm not sleeping with you." She blurted out.

I was surprised by her bluntness. "I have no intentions of fucking you tonight." A smirk crossed my face.

"Look, just because we are getting married doesn't give you a free pass to my body." She said.

"That's exactly what it does give me. We will be mated in the traditions of the Moon River Pack. I trust you have done your research with our mating rituals?"

"Of course I have. I have no plans to break any of the Moon River Pack's laws. We will fuck, as you so eloquently put it during our mating ceremony." I snapped.

"Let's start over." He offered his hand.

I stared at his large hand for a few seconds before I placed mine in it. "Hello, I'm Keyla. I'm a wolf shifter, thirty years old. I love long runs in the forest, cheap wine, expensive whiskey, and a great burger."

He squeezed my hand and grinned. "Nice to meet you, Keyla. I'm Zev. I'm also a wolf shifter, forty years old. My passions include long runs, craft beer, fine whiskey, and a good burger, though I adore a rare steak."

"So, we have a few things in common." I chuckled and removed my hand from his.

"Seems we do." He agreed. "Did you leave a job to move here?"

My head shook. "I am a freelance photographer. I had a studio within the pack compound. I fully intend to pay my way. I'll get a job if need be."

He held up his hand and shook his head. "There is no need for you to work outside of something you love. If photography gives your joy, then the money will come and if, for whatever reason, it doesn't, I make more than enough to provide for you and our nephew."

"What do you do in the pack?" I asked.

"Special Agent in Charge, SBI. Shifters Bureau of Investigation." He said.

I knew what he did. I'm not sure why I asked. Zev made me nervous and off my game. He made me feel things. Things I never felt before with man.

"How are things in the Shadow pack?" Zev asked.

"Same as usual." I shrugged.

"Everyone's happy with their counsel?" He pushed.

"Are you asking as SBI or my future husband?" I tilted my head and took a sip of my shake.

"Maybe both." Zev said.

"Let's be honest for a moment. My father wants me here to spy. You want me here to extract information you can use against my father? I am here for my nephew. Billy is all that matters to me. I would do whatever was necessary to keep him out of William Volkov's clutches."

"You're right. Billy should be all of our concern. I'm glad he had you these past six months." He said. "How is he doing?"

"He is amazing. Billy is the sweetest boy and so smart and creative." I sighed. "We have to get him away from the compound soon. My father can't be trusted, and the fact he is using me shows how desperate he is. William Volkov is a dangerous man, but when he is desperate, he is deadly."

"The full moon is tomorrow. We can do the ceremony then and we can go to the courthouse today if you'd like to get the legal part finished." He offered.

"I forgot your packs follow society's laws and pack laws. Could we do the legal tomorrow before the mating?" I suggested.

"Of course. I'll set up everything for tomorrow." Zev said.

"Do you know Willa and Raven? They own As The Emerald Turns." I asked.

"Of course. They were really close to Daciana." He said.

"I met them when they came to the compound for the wedding reception. We've become good friends since then. I was hoping to meet them for dinner tonight."

"No problem at all. I'll never dictate what you can and cannot do unless it puts you, Billy, or the pack at risk." He said and reached over and patted my hand.

"Thank you."

He looked at my plate and then at my face. "You ready?"

"Sure."

"You can follow me to my house. Did you park on Dalia?" Zev asked as he tossed thirty dollars on the table.

"Yes." I answered.

He stood and offered me his hand. To my surprise, I placed my hand in his hand. A sense of calm washed over me at his touch.

CHAPTER 3

ZEV LYKOUDIS

*K*eyla glanced around my house and her smile faded as she looked at the forest behind it.

"What's wrong?" I asked.

She shook her head. "Nothing. It's a beautiful home."

"Then what's wrong?" I pressed.

"This is all just becoming too real." She said.

"We don't have much of a choice if we want to keep the peace between our packs." I said.

I felt a little punch in the gut, realizing she wasn't happy to be my bride. She walked up onto my porch and sat on the oversized porch swing. Keyla was beautiful even if she was our enemy's daughter and even when she was lying to me about something.

My hands flexed with the urge to pull her into my arms and demand she tell me what secrets she is keeping. Either demand answers or fuck her on my front porch. Her curves were too tempting. I needed a run before she pushed my self-control.

"I'm going for a run. Would you like to join me?" I asked.

A sad, fearful expression took over her beautiful face. Her amber eyes watered and appeared to glow.

She cracked her neck and sighed. "I do, but I can't."

Keyla closed her eyes and leaned her head against the back of the swing.

"Why?" I asked.

"Punishment." She whispered.

"What are you talking about?" I demanded.

"I shouldn't have said anything." She said.

I waited for a few moments before pressing her to expand on her comment.

"Tell me." I took a step closer to the swing.

She brought her legs up to her chest and wrapped her arms around them. She looked like a child.

"My father caught me trying to leave with Billy. He bound my wolf until you and I finish the mating ceremony."

"He is forcing you to marry me." I snapped.

"We are both being forced to mate. I attempted an escape with Billy to make sure he arrived here. I don't trust my father to allow Billy to live with your pack." She explained.

"He has to if he wants peace."

"I'm not sure he wants peace. I don't trust him and neither should you." She said.

A single tear fell down her cheek. It was impossible for me to stop myself. I leaned in and kissed the tear and let my mouth trail down along her jawline. I breathed in her fresh citrus scent. This was fucked up. I'm rock hard in the worst situations. She was opening up to me about her asshole father and all I could think about was dragging her to bed and not letting her leave for a week.

I pulled away and took a deep breath. "Come on, I'll show you around."

I grabbed her hand and dragged her inside. I gave her the ten-cent tour and ended it in the kitchen.

"It's a lovely home." Keyla said as she took a seat at the island.

"Thank you."

"Did you decorate?" She asked.

I laughed. "No. Mom did. She is an interior designer, but if you don't like it, we can change the house."

She shook her head. "No, I love it."

"What do you do for a living? My father told me you don't live within your pack." I said.

"I'm an elementary teacher. Third grade for the past two years." She said with a small smile.

"Do you want to teach here?" I asked.

The local shifters in Hemlock Valley had a private school for shifters. It was a great way for the young shifters to discover and learn to control their abilities without being treated like monsters.

"I would love to teach again. Alpha Volkov forced me to stop teaching and return to the pack when Raff and Daciana died."

"Is Alpha Volkov threatening you? Marry me or never shift again?" I circled back to her, not being able to shift.

She shrugged. "I volunteered, but after he caught me trying to leave with Billy. Daddy dearest decided to take extra measures to ensure the mating it complete."

Keyla sucked in a breath before she asked. "Why did you suggest getting married?"

"It's my duty as the next alpha to protect our pack from war and to protect Daciana's son." I answered honestly.

"Duty." She snorted. "I'm so sick of duty."

"I could have done worse. Sorry about your luck in mates, but I don't mind this arrangement." I said.

CHAPTER 4

KEYLA VOLKOV

*M*y instincts told me I could trust Zev, but my past made it difficult to listen to them. He scared the hell out of me, but not in the same way my father did. No Zev terrified me, because I knew he had the ability to destroy me. Zev Lykoudis would be my salvation or my destruction. He was my mate. Raff and Daciana's wedding is where I felt it first.

"I don't mind my luck." I whispered.

A muscle in Zev's jaw twitched before he bent down and pressed his lips to mine. He claimed my mouth with such passion; I thought I might pass out. My body responded instantly, waking up my wolf. He devoured my mouth and walked us back against the wall. His hard body pressed into mine and my arms slipped around his neck. I wanted more. I needed more from him, but Zev pulled away.

"Sorry, I got carried away." He said and stepped back.

"At least we know we have chemistry." I teased.

He chuckled. "That we do."

I didn't expect to feel this close to him so soon. It's been a few hours in his company, and I already want to tell him all my secrets.

I turned away from him to clear my head. I was already falling for him. Never had I met a man so kind. It didn't hurt that he was hot.

"Will Alpha Lykoudis ask for Billy to arrive before the mating ceremony?" I asked.

"I'm not sure. We can ask him tonight at our engagement party." He said.

"Engagement party? Is that necessary?"

He shrugged. "My parents' idea, but it is just at Shifters', a local bar and grill. Just a few pack leaders, my siblings, and Willa and Rayven."

"Oh, I like Willa and Rayven. We've kept in touch since Daciana's engagement party." I said.

I was relieved I would know at least two people at the party.

"Great. I have a few errands to run before the party. I'll be back in a couple of hours to pick you up," Zev said as he grabbed his keys.

LATER THAT NIGHT AT SHIFTERS

ZEV LYKOUDIS

KEYLA LOOKED AS IF SHE saw a ghost when she saw her father talking to my mother. "Are you alright?" I asked.

She shivered and wrapped her arms around her waist. "Yes, I just wasn't expecting to see my father here."

"I didn't realize he would be here either."

"Keyla!" Willa called out as soon as she saw us. She rushed over and gave Keyla a hug.

"Willa, it's so good to see you," Keyla said as she hugged her friend back. "Where's Rayven?"

"She'll be here soon. She is just closing up the bookstore." Willa said before she looked at me. "I'm going to kidnap your fiancée for a bit. Give her all the Zev Lykoudis gossip."

"Don't believe a word she says." I chuckled and kissed Keyla on the cheek just as Willa pulled her away.

I watched the duo disappear into the crowd, and an odd sense of pride washed over me. She was my mate. It might be a business arrangement, but there was something between us. Something that has grown immensely in just a few hours. Was this the sign of a true mate?

CHAPTER 5

KEYLA VOLKOV

"*A*lcohol and lots of it," Willa vowed as Rayven walked into Shifters' bar and grill.

"Definitely lots of it." Rayven said. "It's good to see you, Keyla."

It felt nice to see these ladies and have some friendly, familiar faces.

"Let's find a table in this madhouse." I smiled at my friends.

We claimed a booth at the back of the bar. "Are the burgers as great as I've heard?" I asked.

"Well, well, if it isn't Keyla Volkov." I knew that voice too well. I turned to see Veronica Bradley, her head cocked to the side, bleached blonde hair falling past her shoulders. Her smile sent chills down my spine. "It's so good to see you, Key." Her overly fake pleasant voice made my skin crawl.

Why was she here? My high school nemesis. What? I can have a nemesis. She had always done everything in her power to make my life miserable.

"Veronica, what a surprise to see you in Hemlock Valley." A forced smile touched my lips.

"I just couldn't believe you were finally getting married. I just had to see for myself." She laughed. "Zev is quite a catch. We were engaged before his father forced him to marry you."

"It's been less than a minute, and you have already worn out your welcome." Willa rose to stand nose to nose with Veronica.

I could tell Willa was about to do something we would all regret, so I placed my hand on her arm to intervene. "Veronica, like I said, it was nice seeing you again, but let's not do this again anytime soon." I gave my best fake smile. "Have a delightful night," I said, with as much pleasantry as I could muster.

Veronica apparently was not ready to move on from her bitchiness. Like I said, she is evil.

"You should thank your sister's spirit. If not for her death, you wouldn't be marrying such a catch." Veronica sneered.

I laughed, "You should go check your makeup, your jealousy is showing." I rose, not sure what I was going to do, but I made my way out of the booth and stood just a few inches from Veronica. "Things are different now, Veronica. The power you used to have over me is gone. Go back to whatever you were doing before we both regret it." I punctuated each word with an unmistakable warning.

I lifted my hand to scratch the corner of my eye, but before my finger made contact, I felt something. No, not something, but someone grabbed my wrist. I swung my head around to see who it belonged to.

"I'd hate it if you were arrested at our engagement party." A voice so deep it made my stomach flip, cautioned.

"She threatened me," Veronica hissed, her face unable to conceal her anger.

"I didn't hear her threaten you, actually I believe it was the other way around." Rayven added.

Veronica glared at my friend before turning her attention toward Zev. "She would have attacked me if you did not arrive."

Willa spoke up. "No, she wasn't. She should have, but she didn't."

"Zevy," Veronica purred, apparently trying to change tactics to get her way.

"I was going to scratch my eye, not hit anyone." I struggled to pull my wrist free, but it just caused him to tighten his grip. "Will you let go of me?" I asked.

"No." He replied flatly.

"Don't let her go; she attacked me," Veronica whined.

"Veronica, she didn't attack you, but I need to talk to my fiancée in private."

He pulled me away from Veronica and my friends. "You and I have things to talk about." He said to me.

"Let go of me," I demanded, continuing to yank my arm from his grasp.

"Stop, you're going to hurt yourself," Zev growled. Dragging me out the back door of Shifters.

"Then let go," I hissed back. I was still pulling my arm and cursing him when we made it outside.

"You got a wild one there, Zev, need any help?" A guy leaning up against the wall, smoking a cigarette, chuckled.

Zev ignored the man. "I will let go if you promise to talk to me like an adult."

"I'm acting like an adult, but you might have warned me your formal fiancée would be at our engagement party."

He snorted. "She is not my former anything. Her father tried to set up an arranged marriage two years ago. I said no then."

"I don't think she would agree." I snapped.

He released my wrist and took a step back. Part of me wanted to run, but I knew he would just chase me. I might as well get this over with.

"Are you jealous?" He looked as if he didn't mean to ask that question, but he didn't take it back or say anything else.

I stepped back, and cursed inwardly, at the feel of the brick wall at my back. Trapped. "Why would I be jealous? It's not like we are really mates."

His hand went to my cheek. "Liar." He said, the heat of his body making it impossible to breathe.

Shit, shit, shit. I had to snap out of this trance. I couldn't fall even harder for him.

He grabbed my hand and pulled me toward the door. Zev dragged me down a hall into a backroom. He locked the door and pushed me against the wall. He kissed me like his life depended on it.

"This is a bad idea, Zev," I whispered yelled.

"Why?" Zev asked, slipping his hand under my dress.

"Because we're in the backroom of a bar," I reminded him. "We aren't mated yet."

"I can't wait and neither can you." He replied against my lips. "I need to be inside you to survive this evening. You need me inside of you."

He was right. Gods, he was right. I needed this just as much as he did. He gave me a deep kiss and then lifted my dress and turned me towards the mirror. With his hand in the middle of my back, he pushed me to lean over a table and commanded. "Lean over."

I was relieved that at least the backroom was away from the main area of the bar. Glancing up at my reflection in the glass of a window, I felt his erection press against my lace-covered backside. I looked wanton and my tits were on the verge of spilling out of my dress. As I met his gaze in the window, my eyes dilated.

"This is foolish. Anyone could hear us or walk in." I said.

Zev pressed his body against mine, his breath hot on my neck. "I don't give a fuck. I need to be inside of you before I explode," he hissed. "And I locked the door." He winked.

His hand slipped under my underwear and pushed them aside, exposing my wet and swollen pussy lips.

"You're so fucking wet," he murmured. He removed my panties from my feet and positioned himself behind me.

"What are you doing to me? This isn't me," I panted.

Zev couldn't resist the urge any longer and thrust himself deep inside me, causing my body to tremble with pleasure. All my protests left the moment his cock was inside of me.

"Tilt your head back. I need to taste you as I fuck you." He demanded.

I looked over my shoulder and saw his eyes, which burned with fire. He yanked down the front of my dress and grabbed my tits, pinching my nipples hard. This caused my pussy to spasm. He felt amazing inside of me. He claimed my mouth in an all-consuming kiss as he fucked me relentlessly.

"You feel so good," he growled, against my lips, the sound almost animalistic. "How do I feel inside of you?"

I could not respond; I simply moaned and tightened my muscles around him, squeezing his dick. Despite the pain in my hips from being pounded into the table, I was about to cum. I didn't want this to end. Right now, I didn't give a fuck if the entire bar heard us.

"Yes, fuck yes," I chanted.

His handsome face looked like the wolf he was as his cock swelled inside of me. He was close, and so was I.

"More," I cried.

He pounded into me, savagely ravaging my pussy. "Mine, tell me you're mine," he demanded, slamming into me over and over again. "Keyla," he warned when I didn't reply, slowing his movements.

"Yes, I'm yours," I said, desperate to climax.

"That's right, Keyla," he purred. He continued to thrust a few more times, and I exploded in ecstasy. "Your body's mine. Your heart's mine too."

"Yes." I moaned honestly.

"And I'm yours." He said as we both collapsed against the table, panting heavily.

When we caught our breath, he turned me in his arms. We stayed like that for several moments before he broke our trance.

He smiled and kissed my nose. "Let's get you cleaned up, mate."

After a few minutes, we left the backroom. Even though it felt like everyone was staring at us, no one said anything.

CHAPTER 6

ZEV LYKOUDIS

*K*eyla had been gone too long to get a drink. My wolf demanded I track her down. He had become more demanding in the last hour since being inside of Keyla. The sound of a gruff male voice cut through the dark hall, hurling insults at Keyla. He called her a half-breed that no pack wanted and claimed she was lucky he let her stay within his pack. The disgusting slurs Alpha Volkov slung at Keyla had my stomach churning with anger, and my wolf growled in protest and demanded to be released.

As I rounded the corner, the scene came into view. Alpha Volkov had Keyla pinned against the wall, and her head bounced off it with a sickening thud. My heart raced as I charged forward, my fists clenched in fury. The sound of my footsteps echoed in my ears as I was closing the distance between us.

The smell of sweat and fear filled the air. I barely made out Keyla's scream when my fist hit her father's face. Blood sprayed from his nose, and he stumbled backward, grasping at the wall for support. But I wasn't finished. I continued to pummel him blow after blow, the sound of my knuckles connecting with his flesh reverberating in my ears.

Finally, he fell to the ground in a whimpering heap, and I stepped back, panting. The adrenaline rush ebbed, and the stench of blood filled my nostrils. My hands shook with anger as I looked down at the beaten man, my heart still pounding in my chest. My wolf wanted more blood.

"Zev?" Keyla's voice was soft, and it pulled my attention away from the asshole lying on the floor. I could hear her breathing, shaky and uneven. I could sense the tension in her muscles as she glanced at her father on the ground.

"Are you okay?" Slowly approaching her, I noticed her eyes widen in fear.

I could feel my heart pounding in my chest as I reached out to touch her, my hand hovering just above her shoulder. "I would never hurt you, Keyla." The thought that I might be the cause of her fear was unbearable.

"He's going to kill me," she said in a panicked voice.

"Never. I won't let him hurt you again," I assured her, surprised at my own bold statement. But I meant every word. As long as I was alive, no one would hurt her again.

I place my hand at the small of her back and lead her towards the exit. She seems dazed, and I'm worried about the extent of the damage her father might have caused.

The cool breeze hit us as we step outside, and I can feel the relief in Keyla's body as she takes a deep breath. The cold air is a welcome change from the fear and tension inside.

"Is he alive?" Keyla asked, her voice still shaky as I guided her to my truck.

"Yes. Why didn't you tell me?" I asked.

"About what? My father beats me or that I'm half human?" She sighed.

"All of it. It doesn't matter to me that you are half human. My wolf recognizes you as its mate." I said.

"And the man?" She asked.

"The man knows you are it for me. Initially, I sensed it upon our first encounter. But I remained fixated on my responsibilities and personal issues. I didn't allow myself to be open to it." I explained.

KEYLA VOLKOV

MY SENSES COME ALIVE, AND I become acutely aware of my surroundings. A tingling sensation overcame me as I realized I just had sex in a bathroom. My father attacked me at my engagement party, and my soon to be husband just beat the crap out of my father.

Zev is a formidable presence. It's not just his muscular build or the tattoos that adorn his arms. There's a certain aura about him that warned you not to fuck with him. Despite this, I am comforted by his presence. My wolf is comforted by his wolf.

As we drive down the road, I can hear the hum of the engine and the sound of the tires on the pavement. The air smells of gasoline and oil, mixed with the scent of the forest that surrounds us. I notice the way the moonlight filters through the trees, casting shadows on the ground.

Despite my fear, I can feel my wolf stirring inside of me, responding to the energy emanating from Zev. It's a strange and thrilling sensation, one that I have never experienced before. I am both frightened and excited by the prospect of what might happen next. As we continue down the road, I try to focus on my breathing, calming my nerves and preparing myself for whatever lies ahead.

He hastily reaches for his phone. He taps on the screen. "Dad, yes, I fucking know about Alpha Volkov on the floor. He's lucky he's still breathing," Zev snarled. "I'll explain everything later. I'm heading to my place tonight with Keyla.

And Dad, we need to get Billy out of Volkov's clutches ASAP."

"You shouldn't talk on the phone while driving," I said, my voice shaky. "Doesn't your truck have Bluetooth?"

He glanced at me, his eyes piercing and intense. "That is your concern?" he asked, his tone laced with frustration.

"I mean," I said, my words stumbling out in a rush, "you just beat up my father for hurting me. It would really suck if all of that effort went to waste, and we ended up crashing."

Zev's head fell back on his shoulders, and he laughed. His laughter was contagious because I started laughing. I couldn't remember the last time I had laughed.

My heart raced as we drove further out of town. I felt the anticipation and anxiety of what was to come. My palms were sweaty, and my body trembled. I felt like I was at a crossroads in my life, not knowing which way to turn. The power Zev seemed to quickly gain over my body and mind was overwhelming and a little scary. But I couldn't deny it the pull.

"How are you feeling right now?" Zev asked, his eyes focused on the road.

I swallowed hard. "Overwhelmed," I muttered.

He chuckled. "I meant are you in pain but overwhelmed makes sense, sweetheart."

I could feel my cheek turn red. I took a deep breath. "No more pain than usual." I muttered and turned to look out the window.

I heard him growl, but I ignored the anger penetrating from him.

"Keyla, try to get some sleep before we reach our place."

Our place. I hope this wasn't another one of my mistakes.

CHAPTER 7

KEYLA VOLKOV

I've been staying with Zev for about a month now. It felt natural to be with him from the beginning. I've never been drawn to any man like this before. It felt more primal, earthy, instinctual.

My wolf was finally waking up, and it was desperate for his wolf. But it wasn't just my wolf that craved Zev. I wanted him too.

"He'll be home tonight." Zev reminded me once again.

Stepping closer to him, I wrapped my arms around his waist and tilted my head back to look into his handsome face. I can't believe how quickly I adjusted to touching and flirting with Zev. I've never felt so at ease with a man before, but with him it's almost like its instinct.

"I know. I wasn't thinking about Billy this time." I said.

Zev smirked. "Oh? What's on your pretty little mind?"

I stepped up on my toes and kissed him. Slipping my tongue through his lips, my arms wrapped around his neck. Our tongues danced together, exploring.

Zev pulled me closer into his hard frame and broke our kiss. "Fuck, I need to fuck you."

I pushed back from him. "We have a little time." I smirked and quickly went to work, freeing his cock from his jeans and sunk to my knees. His thick cock bounced in front of my face.

"We don't have enough time for what I want to do to you." He growled.

I looked up at Zev and slipped my tongue from my lips. I met his gaze and swirled my tongue around the tip of his cock, sliding down the length and back up. "We have time for this." I cupped his balls and gently massaged them. Zev groaned, and it excited me to know I had this effect on him. I took his cock fully into my mouth, flattening my tongue along the underside as he pushed deeper. I gagged when he hit the back of my throat, but quickly recovered. Relaxing my throat muscles, he went further.

"Fuck, Keyla." He growled. His fingers threaded through my hair and tightened at the scalp. I was just gathering my rhythm when the doorbell caused me to jump, and I tried to pull away, but Zev refused to let me move. "Finish what you started, Keyla." He hissed. "They can wait until I cum down your pretty little throat." Zev took over, fucking my face brutally. I loved it.

I did my best to match his movements, and I squeezed my throat muscles around his length, massaging him with each powerful thrust. One last snap of his hips and he shot his seed down my throat. He was breathing heavily, but he didn't leave my mouth. I continued to worship his cock, licking and sucking as the last of his seed coats my throat.

I laughed as the doorbell turned into pounding. My cheeks heated even more when he slipped from my mouth.

He helped me to my feet. "Let's go get our boy." Zev kissed me deeply before he went to the door.

THE SHIFT

KEYLA

ZEV'S HOUSE HAD A LARGE wooded area behind it. We stood at the edge of his property in front of the tree line. I was so nervous I haven't tried since the night of our mating ceremony and I couldn't shift then. What if I couldn't shift again?

"How do you do it?" I asked him.

He looked over at me and shrugged. "My wolf lets me know when he is ready to surface."

"What if I can't shift again?" I whispered, my arms wrapped around my waist.

"We will deal with that if it happens." He squeezed my shoulder. "Billy is with dad, the woods are empty. No pressure. If you can't shift, then you can't shift. No big deal."

Yeah, easy for him to say. I've felt my wolf more lately. Maybe I could do it without.

"Let's try." I said.

"Relax and think about your wolf. Talk to her, ask her to surface. Tell her it's safe and you want to run." He suggested.

I took a deep breath and tried to find a path to my wolf. She felt stronger, but she wasn't shifting. "Maybe if she sees your wolf, she'll feel more comfortable." I suggested.

"Maybe." He strips out of his clothes, and I watch as his body started to contort. Fur appears on his arms, then he is on all fours. More hair, more shifting until a beautiful black wolf is in front of me.

He leans against my legs, and I instinctually pat his head. His fur is soft and thick. My wolf is stirring. "Come on, girl, come meet Zev's wolf. You two can run together."

After removing my dress from my head, I threw it to the ground along with my bra and panties. I kicked off my shoes and went to the ground. I nuzzled Zev's wolfy neck. My wolf was scratching my belly. She wanted to shift.

I saw reddish fur form on my arms. My muscles tightened and flexed. I was shifting. It hurt. Pain wracked through my body as I shifted. Zev's wolf sat on his hind legs and howled as I transformed into my wolf.

He bumped my side with his head and took off running into the woods. My wolf chased after him. He was playing with me, dipping in and out of thick trees and over fallen limbs. I was laughing inside as I ran faster. I finally felt strong and free.

I was free.

HEMLOCK VALLEY

LEPRECHAUN CAUGHT MY TONGUE

SKYLAR QUINN

CHAPTER 1

Jacob Martin — Sandwich Shop — E. Dalia Street — March 16th

*T*here was a saying in the demon world: better to hide in plain sight than to hide in fear of being caught. That's what I had done my whole life: lived in plain sight. Being a few centuries old had its ups and downs, but one thing was certain: the older you were, the easier it was to deal with the humans. You learned to cope with their weird habits and needs -or instance, the need to dress up on certain days of the year. Why Halloween and St Patrick's day have become infused with candy and meaningless items is beyond my comprehension. I remember when these holidays meant something special.

When I was a teenage demon in the late 12th century, the kids thought dressing up fooled us. But it didn't. We just enjoyed walking among everyone without fear of exorcisms.

Now, we're dressing up our shops in shamrocks and little leprechauns. Some of my vampire friends tell me I have become a sour old man. But it's more than that. Humans don't appreciate where these traditions came from and what it took for them to develop.

That's the curious thing. You wouldn't think me, Jacob Martin, a demon, would appreciate something like Saint Patrick's Day. But I do. Because if you believe in what Patrick did all those years ago, then it means you believe in demons too. And that's where our powers come from.

With everyone celebrating the candy aspect of these holidays, our powers diminish. And that's just not something I can keep living with. I'm too old to watch the powers my family gave me dry up. I had to do something. I was heading to As The Emerald Turns book store after work today. I knew one of those two owners could help me with what I was looking for.

My lunch break was almost over, and I knew I had more customers about to walk in, so I cleaned up my sandwich scraps and pushed my thoughts to the back of my mind. It was time to throw on the smile for everyone in Hemlock Valley who needed a good lunch in the middle of their day.

I walked out of my office and back into the front of the restaurant. I bought this sandwich shop two decades ago when I learned about this town. It's been great for the most part, except for all these blasted human traditions.

"Hey Jacob," Sharon, the head waitress, called my name.

"Yeah?"

"Some guy at the front counter is asking for you."

I looked over at the counter, and it wasn't just some guy; it was the town's mayor. Mayor William Thompson, our resident demi-god. *Great. This was going to be about the damn parade tomorrow.*

"Thanks Sharon, I'll go talk to the mayor."

Walking through my sandwich shop, I always took pride in the work of my employees. We ran a tight ship; everyone kept to their duties and our facilities were always clean. It made for a nice work/life balance.

"Mayor Thompson," I said, giving the best fake smile I could.

"Jacob."

We shook hands like the men on Earth did when greeting one another and then got to business.

"You don't have a float in the parade tomorrow," William said.

"Nope. Didn't know I had to."

"No one 'has to,'" he said in air quotes. "But you know how much the kids enjoy all the shops getting involved."

I leaned in and lowered my voice. "William, you and I both know what B.S. this whole thing is. It's all a candy company whoopla now. Not at all what it was meant for back in the day."

"Be that as it may, Jacob, you know I work very hard to keep our town's image up. What would they think if our local sandwich joint didn't partake?"

I smirked. "That we were too busy to close for the morning?"

"Not a soul in the town will think that since we will all be at the parade. Come on, Jacob. This will be good for your demon spirit. Give the big guy something to get on your case about. I know how much he hates it when you bond with the humans."

My eyes rolled at the sound of his comment about Satan, but it was hard to argue with him. His demi-god status made him the top dog in this state, and I didn't feel like arguing.

"What if I just provide snacks for everyone? Like a table with sandwiches for everyone to grab free of charge?"

"You would rather go through all that effort than the float?" he asked.

I nodded my head. "Yup."

He grinned. "Perfect. I'll accept the gracious offer. Thanks Jacob. See you bright and early."

"How early?" I asked.

"Nine sharp."

I watched His Highness walk out of my shop and realized that to make this possible, I would need to take part of the afternoon off to head to As The Emerald Turns to do my research.

"Hey Sharon," I called out, walking over to where she was standing. "You still looking for any overtime?"

"Always. You know those kids are bleeding me dry at home."

"We are going to be sponsoring a snack table for the parade. We have to set up at nine sharp, which means the food needs to be prepped and made tonight or early tomorrow. What time is your shift over today?"

"I'm off in an hour, so plenty of time to prep whatever you want for the parade."

"Plan on making 200 sandwiches to be cut into quarters. Then we will need to decorate a table. How much time do you think you will need for that?"

Sharon thought for a moment. "I can make the sandwiches in five hours tonight, and then I can stop by the store on the way home today and start setting up around 7 am tomorrow."

I pulled my wallet out of my pocket and handed her my company credit card. "Perfect. Use my card for whatever you need. I need to run some errands and will be back later on.

"My pleasure, Jacob. Thanks for the overtime."

I nodded my head at her and then walked out of my shop. Raven and Willa's bookstore was right next door. I would need to do my research now to be ready for tomorrow.

CHAPTER 2

Jacob Martin — As The Emerald Turns — E. Dalia Street

*W*hen I pushed open the door to the bookstore, I was caught off guard by the overabundant smell of magic that permeated the air. This was what I needed. Magic.

"Willa, it's Jacob," Raven said as she smiled in my direction. "You were right. He showed up right on time."

I hated it when the witch did that. I smiled at Raven. "Hello. Is she taking visitors right now?"

Raven smiled. "She's been expecting you." I watched as she pointed across the bookstore to a room in the back.

"Thanks." Traveling through the rows of old books, I let myself pause a moment and appreciate the scents in the room. There was old magic within these walls.

"Jacob," Willa said as she greeted me at the door. "Please come sit down."

"It's creepy when you don't act surprised when you receive visitors."

She grinned; it was a sexy grin, but I swore off witches for a year. The last time I fell for a sexy grin on a witch I regretted it for a month. "We do it to mess with you."

"I know."

"What I don't know, Jacob, is why you are here. What are you looking for?"

"The long and short of it is that my demonic powers are dying, and I need to catch a leprechaun, force it into servitude, and have it regenerate my powers."

"I can't help you enslave another creature. That goes against my beliefs." She looked around the room and then back at me. "But why a leprechaun?"

"Haven't you heard that if you catch one, you can force it to give you a wish? My wish will be to feed my powers for the rest of my existence."

"They aren't genies." Willa shook her head and then walked over to a shelf and pulled a book down. "I think this one will help you. It talks about where your powers come from and what you can do to replenish them."

"So, to clarify, you will not help me do this?"

Willa shook her head. "No Jacob, I won't. But I will give you this book to help you better understand what's going on and what you can do to work on restoring what's been lost."

I graciously took the book, thumbed through it, and frowned. "I wish you could help me with more. But I appreciate this very much."

"You know, if it was within my powers to do more, I would have."

Extending my hand to Willa, "I know. Thank you."

As I walked out of the bookstore, I heard Raven say, "He really looks great as he leaves the store, doesn't he?"

That made me smile. No matter how many centuries I have been alive, there is nothing like an empowered woman of modern times. They knew what they wanted, when they wanted it, and how they wanted it. It was a wonderful time to be alive. Sexually, that was.

I popped back into my shop and walked to my office before anyone could stop me. I now had a mission. Somewhere in this book, there was the answer to my issues. I knew this because I could smell the powers wafting off the pages of this book.

It was an original grimoire, and I knew Willa had to be certain it held the key to my replenishment. I just needed to find it.

~

*A*FTER SEVERAL HOURS OF READING through the grimoire of a witch from the fifteenth century, I finally thought I had landed on the spell that I needed. It wasn't specific to leprechauns, but it was for mythical creatures.

There would be a price I had to pay, which was always the case with magic. There were no free rides in the spiritual realm.

I wasn't sure if humans or even witches would think to use this spell for a leprechaun, since so many of them were gone. They had become folklore instead of being celebrated for the powerful fairies they really were. But I could complete this spell tonight, and hopefully, by morning, I wouldn't need to keep relying on the generosity of our esteemed mayor for my safety.

There was a light knock on the door, which caused me to bring the payroll books across my desk and place them on top of the grimoire.

"Come in," I said.

Sharon walked inside my office, grinning. "I have good news and bad news."

"It worries me with that smile you have."

"Because you're a smart man," she laughed.

"Bad news first."

"The canopy has a hole in it, and I didn't know if you wanted me to replace that tonight for tomorrow's activities."

I sighed. "That's it? Yes, take care of that. Just buy a new setup. I don't want to waste time removing the material and putting it back on the metal frame. You know how much I hate that damn thing. Now the good news."

"Sandwiches are done. It only took four hours. So, I'm off to do the shopping."

A relief, I smiled. "I'll pay you for six to cover your shopping time. See you in the morning. And Sharon, if I haven't said it lately, thank you."

"Thanks, Jacob. You know, for a demon, you really have a kind heart when you want to."

I smirked. "Not many people know I'm a demon."

Sharon laughed. "Few nowadays know what an ancient grimoire is either, but we all have our secrets."

I looked down at my desk and then back at her. "I didn't realize you were a witch."

She shook her head. "Not a witch. I'm a phoenix. I like that I can blend in with the humans, and no one knows a thing. But I've lived a long time. Let me know if you need help with whatever you're up to."

"Are your children also phoenixes?" My sudden curiosity took me off guard.

Sharon smiled. "Ruby is. She's so eager to have her first rebirth."

"And Thomas?" It surprised me that I remembered her son's name.

"No," her face dropped in sadness. "Sadly, he is a human, like his father, and both Ruby and I will have to mourn them one day."

"I'm sorry." This shot of reality was hard to hear, but it was a good lesson that everyone in this town had some sort of demon they were facing, even if it wasn't an actual demon. "Thanks again, Sharon. Why don't you take home a pie for the family, too?"

"Goodnight Jacob and thank you."

As Sharon closed my door, I pushed the payroll books off the grimoire and looked over the instructions. I had some preparations to get under way.

CHAPTER 3

Jacob Martin — His Home — Shifter Lane

*T*he clock had just struck eleven, and I had gathered all the supplies I needed to perform this ancient magic. Hopefully, there was still enough energy to pull from so I could tap into the ley lines nearby. It had been almost a century since I had performed this type of work. Honestly, I didn't think it was something I would ever pursue; otherwise, I would have paid more attention when my mother taught it to me. Guess offspring ignoring their parents transferred to all types of creatures on this planet, not just humans.

Hemlock Valley was close enough to Salem that the ley lines were easy to feel. It was tapping into them that would be the hard part. I hadn't traveled or used them in a century. I had always been taught they would remember your signature. Suppose this would be the ultimate test.

The instructions noted the type of salt circle to form. I was in my basement, which seemed like the safest place to perform this ridiculous last-minute effort. I laid out an eight-foot circumference circle, and inside it I drew a pentagram with chalk. Six-inch-thick candles were at each of the tips of the pentagram. I had enough magical ability that lighting a candle would still be considered a parlor trick for me.

Once the room was set, I shut the lights out, stood on the outside of the circle, and focused on the chant I had spent an hour memorizing. My eyes shut, my arms went out, my elbows touching my sides as my palms were open and face up. In many ways, I felt like I did as a child, excited and anxious to play with magic again. But the other part of me knew that with balance, the price I would end up paying may be steep. As a demon, part of the balance that God had bestowed on us wasn't determined until the end of the action. So, whatever I did once I had the leprechaun would impact the price my soul paid. *Didn't you just love those extra punches the almighty creator bestowed on his demonic sons and daughters?*

Focusing my energy and attention back to the moment at hand, I closed my eyes and let my mind relax. The ley lines sang to me. Maybe it was just like riding a bicycle. My skin started to crawl as I let my mind travel into the ley lines, and when enough energy filled me, I started on the chant. Another fun fact about using the ley lines was that the charge we received from them was erotic in nature. It took a lot of practice to keep one's mind focused on the task instead of wandering off into the many, many thoughts that began popping into your mind for as long as you were inside the lines.

Chanting wasn't my strong suit or something I loved, especially while aroused. It was one of the main reasons why I didn't do it often. But it was coming relatively easily at the moment. The feelings and sensations weren't as overpowering as I had remembered them. As I went into the last line of the chant, I felt the room vanquish all heat inside of it, and the cold that took over was turning my blood to ice. It was a powerful and unnerving sensation that reminded me why I had preferred easier magic to the more complex.

When the final word was said, the candle lights extinguished, and after a few moments, I thought I must have messed something up. The candles were supposed to relight automatically. My body stood still, and I stopped breathing as I focused on the waxed objects. Moments passed and then I heard the flickering start, and the flames returned.

I was no longer alone in my basement. Standing before me was a light brown haired, pale-skinned fairy covered in green dust. She had to be close to six feet tall, was naked, and had legs for days.

There was no telling what I had done wrong. Maybe I brought back a water sprite instead of a leprechaun. The words in Gaelic could have been pronounced wrong. But there we stood, eye to eye, looking at one another. I felt my cock hardening, a wonderful after effect of the ley lines. Hell, that wasn't what I needed right now. This creature in front of me was gorgeous to look at and I knew that I needed to speak. Standing there gaping at a naked creature wasn't polite or productive, no matter the culture or breed.

"Hi," I said in my demonic natural language. It caught me off guard that I would speak that dialect. Not English or even the Gaelic was used to summon her.

She blinked at me a few times and walked towards me. I knew she was unable to break out of the salt circle. When she spoke, it was the most sultry and seductive voice I had ever heard.

"Hello, Master. How may I be of service to you."

Shit, maybe I summoned a genie after all.

"My name is Jacanobich," I said. *Wow, I said my actual demonic name.* "But you can call me Jacob."

"My name is Patromachiy, but you can call me Patty."

"You can understand me?" I asked her in wonderment.

She nodded. "Yes, I can speak all of the languages of those I encounter. You're hearing me in English, but I am speaking your native tongue."

"How do you know I can hear you in English?"

Patty smiled. "I know a lot of things, Jacanobich. I also know that your body wants to bond with mine." She parted her legs as she stood in front of me. Her hands traveled up and down her body. "I'm willing to let you, if that's your wish."

I gulped, "Are you a genie?"

Her head shook back and forth. "You intended to summon a leprechaun, didn't you?"

I nodded. "I expected a short, ugly green man."

Her laughter filled the room and instead of worrying me more, it eased my anxiety. "Would you prefer I bring you my father?"

"Hell, no."

She smiled. "Good. Now, where should we begin?"

CHAPTER 4

Jacob Martin — His Home — Shifter Lane

My eyes were locked onto Patty's body as her hands continued to run along her skin. She was one of the most breath-taking creatures I had ever laid eyes on, and I didn't know what to do about that. I could feel my mouth watering as I became transfixed by her. The green dust that shook off her skin as she moved made everything even more arousing. I wanted to run my tongue over her body and consume her in every possible way.

"I don't understand how I summoned you and not your father," I finally said. "I need a full fledged leprechaun. Not a half-breed of whatever your mother was." Hearing my words as I spoke sounded harsh, but I didn't know how to say it in my native tongue otherwise.

"We can switch to English if you prefer those words," Patty responded.

"You knew I was struggling with word choice?" Now I was even more captivated.

She nodded. "I am a full breed leprechaun. But you summoned me in the middle of my preparation spell for our most holy of days.

"That's why I did it. I needed a powerful leprechaun to help me."

Patty nodded her head again. "Jacanobich, what did you need?"

"Please call me Jacob. And I need help to ensure my demonic powers never fade away again."

She shook her head back and forth. "Sorry, Jacob. I can't help you with that. That isn't in our wheelhouse."

My eyes still transfixed on her body as her hand was now moving back and forth on the outside of her nether regions. She even had the lightest green pixie hair on the base of her pubic region. It became harder and harder to focus. "Are you sure you're not a succubus?" I laughed.

Patty smiled. "Do you want to let me seduce you, Jacob?"

I felt my head nod without me even giving the command. She stepped to the edge of my salt circle. She put her hand palm up, pressed against the invisible wall of our safety circle right next to my cock. I felt it jump and grow even more. Was she controlling it?

Heat suddenly flooded my body, and I needed to remove my clothing. My hands reached for my pants, and I unbuckled them and pushed them to the ground. My cock was fully erect, and instinct wanted me to step against the barrier and let her hand grab me.

"Wait, no," I said, shaking my head and looking down at my cock. "You're tricking me."

She smiled at me with a smile that would make you die for her. "No, I'm seducing you."

"I know what will happen the moment I break that salt barrier. I may be old and horny, but I'm not stupid."

Patty grinned. Her face looked magical, and I could

picture her on her knees, my cock in her mouth, my body fucking her pretty little head harder and harder.

"What if I promise not to hurt you?"

I laughed out loud, "You can't hurt me, little fairy. I'm a demon."

She shook her head. "A demon in need of a power recharge. I can't offer you endless power, but I can recharge you for a short time."

"How long?" I thought about the question I asked and realized I had asked the wrong one. "And how much would this cost me? What kind of magic is it?"

"We can call it a trade. Mating with your kind would give me enough of a boost that would allow me to break free of my family binding. I wouldn't be limited to traveling via rainbows anymore or depend on being summoned to leave."

"Sounds like this is an even trade you're proposing?"

The way her head nodded slowly made me know she was keeping something back.

"What aren't you telling me?"

I caught my hand moving to my cock. The urge to stroke myself was becoming overpowering. Her sexual presence was intense, and I had felt nothing like this before.

"What you would give me would be permanent. What I would give you would not be."

"You could have lied. Why tell the truth?"

Patty shook her head. "I don't lie. I may play tricks and be ornery, but I won't outright lie."

I considered her proposal and before I responded to it, my hand seemed to do the talking for me. My fingers were wrapped around my thick cock, stroking my shaft. I watched her own hand mirror my motions in a way. Her fingers were now on her pussy, spreading her lips and teasing her own sweet cunt.

"Fuck, damn it," I bellowed.

"What's wrong, Jacob?"

"Fine, you have a deal." I spoke. "But, on one condition."

She grinned, tilted her head, and waited.

"I decide when we're finished."

Patty removed her fingers from her pussy, extended her arm, and reached for me like she wanted a handshake. "Deal."

Once again, my hand responded for me. My arm mirrored her movements and when our hands locked, a force-field of magic erupted in my basement, sending both of us across the room in two separate directions, landing on our bare asses.

"Oh my, this is going to be fun," she said with the most wicked and sinister laugh I had ever heard.

What had I gotten myself into?

I watched as she stood up and walked over to me. Her hips swayed as if she was a professional runway model.

"Now that terms are agreed on, payment is due."

Still on my back, I looked up at her as she towered over me. Her legs parted and I could see her green pubic hair outlining her pussy. My cock ached; it was so hard. She lowered her body. I watched her knees bend, her legs spread, and her pussy consume my cock.

"Oh fuck," I moaned out loud as she slid down my cock. "You're so fucking tight!"

"The first time is always tricky."

"Wait, what? First time?" I protested.

Patty silenced any objections as she placed her mouth on mine. Her lips tasted so sweet. Her skin was soft, and my body let instinct take over. There was no more thinking, no more cares in the world. Right at this moment, I was taking the virginity of this leprechaun and nothing else mattered. When I felt her teeth tease my tongue, my body shivered. Literally, this leprechaun caught my tongue. My hands roamed along her body, caressing her skin and teasing my own senses.

"Oh, god," I heard her moan as she slowly, almost at a

gingerly pace, rocked her hips along my shaft. She let me take over control, which was for the best since she was a virgin.

My hands gripped her hips, and I guided her with each motion. I moved my body into a sitting position. Her legs wrapped around my back.

"Take my shirt off," I ordered her.

Her hands ran down my back before grabbing the hem of my shirt and pulling it up and over my head. We were now skin to skin, and it was like the world was on fire. Her green fairy dust was all over me. It was in the air, it was everywhere. I smashed my lips into hers and her hands were on my back. Her nails dug into my skin with each thrust I forced off her hips. There was nothing soft or loving about what I was doing.

"Don't move, just hold on," I said, as I held onto her tightly and maneuvered my way into a standing position.

I walked us up against a stone wall. I was sure it was torturously cold against her back as I held her in place with my weight pressing her into the wall.. One of my hand moved to her breasts It was my turn to do the thrusting. My fingers wrapped around her supple boobs, my head lowered, and I bit into her left nipple. Her moan was almost a scream, which heightened my fun. I moved my hips hard and fast, thrusting in and out of her.

There was a hint of blood in my mouth. I could taste her crimson copper juices as it slowly dripped onto my tongue. It was enough of a reminder to me that I needed to ease up. She was intoxicating, but I had to still be gentle with her. Her body wasn't like mine; she wasn't indestructible.

Releasing her breast from my mouth, I let that hand drop to her ass. I cupped her cheek and held her in place as I got back into my rhythm.

"Amazing, fucking amazing," she moaned.

It was like the whole world was on fire. Everything burned to the touch. But not in a bad way, in a powerful way. The more I worked her over, the hotter her cunt became. She was so wet, eager and ready, it was hard to believe she was a virgin.

"I'm coming!" she cried out.

As her juices flowed over my cock, they ran down my shaft and to my balls. I didn't expect what happened when her juices touched my sack. My body froze and my cock erupted. Years of pent-up angst, aggression and horniness exploded inside of me, releasing through my cock. I could feel my seed painting the insides of her body with my DNA. I had no idea what that would do to a fairy having a demon inside her. That wasn't my concern. My main concern was rejuvenating my powers, and for the first time in centuries, I could feel that happening.

"Holy fuck!" I cried out as literal fire danced over my skin. I quickly pulled my cock out of her, set her down on the ground, and tried to put the fire out on my skin.

"No, don't stop it. Let it work the magic over!" Patty cried out, holding both her hands up at me.

She was controlling the fire, and it was controlling my magic. This was the most amazing thing I had ever experienced, and when the flames vanished, I was left feeling completely whole.

"Are you pleased?" Patty asked with a smile.

I blinked a few times, letting the power soar through my veins before answering. "Hell yeah, I am!"

The sex charged vixen that stood in front of me had a beaming smile on her face. She was proud of her work, and whether she knew it or not, I wouldn't let her go anytime soon.

"I'm starving, are you hungry?" I asked.

"I'm always hungry," she laughed.

"Good, I'll make you some food. We have things to discuss."

I grabbed her hand, pulled her over to the stairs and then up them. We had terms to renegotiate, and I had a feeling she wasn't going to be happy.

CHAPTER 5

Patty — Jacob's Home — Shifter Lane

I looked around the house to take in everything I could. It had never happened before, me being summoned. I heard about it, sure, but never experienced it. The elders of the village made it seem like it would hurt, being ripped away from your home.In reality, it just tingled;the pain was nothing more than a prick you would feel when you get stung by a bee.

"So, you assumed all leprechauns were short, ugly men?" I asked as we moved into his kitchen and sat down at the kitchen table.

He laughed, "I mean, that's what is always advertised."

"You would think a demon would know the difference between fiction and reality," I chuckled.

"Had I known that leprechauns were like you, I would have summoned you a long time ago."

I shook my head. "That's not exactly how it works. Now

that you've summoned me, and we mated, you won't ever be able to summon another one. Only me."

Jacob's eyes opened wide as he looked at me. "Really?"

I nodded, "Really."

My gaze roamed around his kitchen as I looked at everything he had. "How long have you lived as a human?"

"Long enough."

"And you knew your powers were fading?"

I nodded my head.

"Well, I should say they were fading. I am sure you can feel them recharging as we speak."

Jacob held his hands out to look at them. "I can. It is wonderful."

"My pleasure to be of service to you."

"Did you enjoy what I gave you?" Jacob grinned at me.

I couldn't help smirking. "I loved it."

"You're lucky because I have not decided when I would be content letting you go."

"I'm free to go anytime I want."

Jacob shook his head. "No, you agreed to let me decide when we were finished. I don't think we're done yet."

My body tingled hearing his words. I had never felt responses like that before. "You completed your sexual act, I did too. What's left?"

Jacob laughed. "There is so much left. So much! Why, we only did it once!"

I shrugged my shoulders, "Maybe I have been kept a prisoner in my family for far too long. I didn't know there was much more." I grinned at him. Truthfully, I knew there was more, but I have found over the years, in observing other creatures, if you let the men of a species take the lead and "teach', then you're more likely to get what you want.

And I wanted complete freedom from the binds that held me.

Jacob stood up and walked to me, reached his hand out, and expected me to place my hand in his. "Come with me."

"Again?" I smirked.

Doing as he asked, I let him pull me to a standing position and walk me to the back of his house. There I found his bedroom. He had a bright, red-colored comforter with soft tan walls. It seemed like an odd combination.

"Sit," he ordered.

"I didn't know you were bossing me around now."

"Oh, someone is a bit sassy, isn't she?"

My lips curled into a grin. "I don't think you would like a woman who just fell over all your words and didn't have some spunk back."

"You're right, I wouldn't. Now, sit."

He didn't give me an option to disobey. He put his hands on my shoulders and pushed me down onto his bed. It was soft, the comforter was the most exquisite material I had ever felt.

"I'm going to do things to you that you never even imagined."

"There is a lot I have imagined, Jacob."

"Challenge accepted," he grinned before kneeling and looking up at me. "Have you ever been worshipped by a demon?"

He knew the answer. He knew I was a virgin to him. But that didn't stop him. I grinned, watching as he took my foot in his hand and kissed it. His hands massaged the aches and pains of my arch before he started kissing up my leg. When he got to my knee, his hand was tickling me. The laughter couldn't stay contained.

"Stop," I giggled out.

"I need you to promise me something." He said right before he returned to kissing my skin. His mouth moved further up my leg, getting closer and closer to my sweet lucky charms of fun.

"What?"

Jacob shook his head. "Not yet."

When his lips pressed on mine, I felt his tongue slip out and lick my slit. It all felt so warm and exciting.

"Mhmm," I murmured.

"Yeah," he said into my hot cunt. His face dove inside, and it felt like his body was transforming. His tongue was much longer than I had expected it to be.

"Jacob," I moaned.

His hands were now under my ass, and he pulled on my body, my back fell and landed on the mattress. He moved my legs to his shoulders, where my ankles locked. I needed to feel this. It was amazing.

"Enjoy my little leprechaun," he said, as he took a brief break.

We continued like this, his mouth dining on my juices. My body was going into a spasm. Feelings that were not imaginable. He was right, something was happening.

"Dear god," I moaned out louder.

"That's it," he coaxed.

Then suddenly he removed his mouth and his fingers took over. My eyes were shut and all I could do was fade away into the surge of hormones raging through my body and how they were responding to him.

"Patty," he said as he kissed my breasts.

"Mhm?" I responded with.

Nothing seemed to matter as I was falling in love with what he was doing to me to bring out these types of orgasms.

When it finally hit, I released a loud cry as waves of pleasure washed over me, everything being forgotten.

"Stay with me forever," he said. "We can rule earth with your power and mine."

"Yes, yes!" I cried out. I wasn't even sure what he had really asked all I cared about was the orgasm powering over me.

When his cock slid into my wetness, he fit perfectly. He filled every inch of my cavern completely and as he thrust in and out, I responded in kind. My body arched, my breasts pressed against him and together we made magical love over and over on his bed in the most passionate way.

"Jacob!" I screamed out.

"Yes," he said.

"Finish me now, please!"

People had discussed sexual acts as transactional and basic, but nothing like this. Nothing like this mind-blowing world changing experience. It was scary and mesmerizing all at the same time.

As he collapsed on me. My breath was heavy. I had never experienced anything like this, and now I didn't want to give it up.

"Thank you," he panted out as he lay on top of me.

"You're welcome." I responded.

"We will do this so many more times," Jacob said with a grin.

"I'll be leaving soon."

He shook his head, "No, you won't. I haven't said we were done. And I just asked you to stay with me forever."

I opened my eyes and looked at him, had he said that? Did I agree to that? "What? Huh?"

"I asked you to stay forever, and you said yes."

Shaking my head, "No, that wasn't the terms. I was responding to the sex with a yes."

It was the demon's turn to shake his head. "I've been dealing with mythological spells for much longer than you have been alive. I asked, you accepted. I successfully renegotiated the terms of our deal."

Pushing him off of me I sat up and looked around. *Was what he said true? Could I never leave?*

"Jacob…" I started to say before he stopped me.

"Don't worry, you won't be kept as a slave or anything.

But you will have expectations as my powers will need recharging. Go shower and find some clothes. The city parade will start in a few hours, we have time to talk about your new life.

CHAPTER 6

Jacob Martin — His Home — Shifter Lane — March 17th

I left Patty in the bedroom as I walked into my kitchen and then over to the living room. This morning had been a wild one. Somehow it was now six in the morning, and I had to get ready for the parade. Really, what I needed was to sit down and think about what I had just done. I had forced another creature into my servitude. It was a very demon thing to do but not a very Jacob thing. So much time had been spent making myself different from other demons that I may have just sent all that away for sex.

But the sex was fucking amazing. I had never been with a woman of any species that responded to me like Patty had. It was going to be a curse and a blessing. I was sure of it.

"What do we do now?" I heard her voice come from the edge of the room.

Quickly turning around, I smiled at her and offered her to sit on the sofa. "Let's talk."

"Okay."

She had found some of my clothes to wear. She looked cute, really cute. I could smell my scent all over her which drove me mad. "I'm sorry," I started with.

"Somehow, I don't think you are." Her retort was warranted. I wasn't really sorry. I mean, I was, but not really.

"I regret that this has to be the case. But you said you couldn't fix me permanently. There is no other way."

"What does this all mean for me, then?" Patty asked.

I shrugged my shoulders. "As a demon, I have never kept anyone before. Of course, most of my demon friends and family have slaves, but that's not what I want from you."

"What is it you're thinking you want then?" Patty had her hands on her arms and was rubbing them up and down.

"Are you cold?"

She nodded. "A bit."

I walked over to the basket I kept blankets in, pulled one out and brought it to her. "I think you will need your own room."

"Thanks, I think." Her response was snarky in a tone, but I knew she was mad.

"I don't intend on making this a hell for you. I live a very human existence. You could live here with me too in Hemlock Valley."

"And do what?" she asked.

"Why not work with me at the sandwich shop? Or at any of the other places around town."

She pulled the blanket around her body, locking herself in a warm cocoon.

"Patty, really, I'm sorry this happened to you. You seem very kind."

"I am kind."

Her words were soft. I felt like such an asshole.

"Can I see my family?"

I thought about her request. "Maybe. We will need to see how things carry out. I can't promise anything right now."

Her silence said so much.

"I have a St. Patrick's Day parade to start tending to. You can stay here in my home or come join me at work. Your pick. But I am going to get ready."

I left the room and went back to my bedroom, showered and got dressed. If she decided to join me, great. If not, I had work to do.

~

Patty—E. Dalia Street

J FOLLOWED JACOB FROM HIS home to his work. I kept my distance, not wanting to bother him. The way he interacted with the other humans around him struck me as fascinating. He was a powerful being. Even more powerful after the two sessions of lovemaking. Why wasn't he flaunting it around his town or making these humans bow down to him?

Clearly, there was more to learn about this demon than I had realized.

I started to walk around the street where the different shops were setting up their booths. They all seemed to love this. There were fake leprechauns everywhere.

It would be my first St. Patrick's Day celebration. My brothers had talked about them all the time when I was a kid. They would travel the rainbows and venture into the human realms for this activity. It did seem like a fun thing to do.

"Hi there," a voice said from behind me.

Turning around, I saw a nice woman looking at me. She was beautiful and had very kind eyes.

"Hi."

"My name is Willa. What's yours?"

"Patty. That's a pretty name."

The stranger grinned at me, "So is Patty. I've never met a leprechaun in real life before."

"How do you know I am one?"

She smiled. "Because I gave Jacob the book that he used to summon you. I felt the magic over night when he cast the spell."

"Oh," I said to her.

"You seem scared. Did he hurt you?"

Shaking my head. "No, of course not. He wasn't scary or hurtful at all."

Willa nodded her head. "Good. He is a kind soul, for a demon."

That made me laugh, the way she said 'for a demon.' "He was really good at sex."

Suddenly, Willa started laughing. "I imagine he would be, having many hundreds of years to practice his technique."

"Oh," I blushed. "That does sound about right. I hadn't thought of that."

"Sorry if this isn't my business. But if he didn't hurt you and you two had good sex, why are you so sad looking?"

This woman was easy to talk to, and she seemed like she was friends with Jacob. I didn't want to talk badly about him to his friend. "It's nothing."

Willa walked up to me, took my hand, and pulled me to her little table. "Here, have some hot cocoa and tell me what's going on."

No one had treated me like this before; they were so welcoming and friendly, like family. I took the hot cocoa and the seat that was offered and started spilling my guts out.

"It's my fault really. I wanted to use him as an end to being trapped with my family. And now I ended up trapped by him. From one enslavement to another."

"From what you just described, it didn't sound so bad, sexually."

"Oh, that part was great. It's the not being in control of my life part that sucks."

"Did Jacob offer you any specifics of what being with him would mean?"

I nodded my head. "He said something about me needing a room and that I could stay in his town with him."

Willa nodded. "Yes, you can stay here. Hemlock doesn't have any leprechauns, and it would be such fun to have another magical being like yourself. I'm a witch, too. There are so many of us scattered all over."

"Is everyone as nice as you?" I asked while sipping some of her cocoa.

"Well, I won't lie. No. There are some major Karens around town. But what's a small town without some gossip jerks? But don't worry, there are more of us than there are of them."

Smiling, "I don't know what I would do with myself all day."

"What do you do at home all day?"

"Read, sometimes write, and I love to play music."

"Then it's settled. You will come to the bookstore with Raven and me. You can work for us and help our customers find the perfect books for their needs."

I was very taken aback. This woman was so nice, offering first friendship and now a job. I didn't know what to say.

"Please say yes. We could use someone like you at our shop."

"Do you get a lot of customers?"

"In person, not really, but we have a huge presence online. There are lots of online shoppers for mythical books and magical artifacts.

As I finished my cocoa, I suddenly realized I felt better. "What was in this drink?"

"You can feel it?" Willa asked.

Nodding, "Yes, very peaceful."

"I said a peace blessing over it for comfort and enjoyment as I brewed it. Glad to hear it worked for you!"

"Are all of you magical?"

She shook her head. "No, there are plain Jane humans scattered around, but most of us are paranormal to some degree. We all love it and are open with it. The humans think it is a tourist attraction."

"Oh, so you just hide in plain sight?"

She grinned. "I knew you were smart."

"Yes, thank you. I would love to help you and your partner at the bookstore on a part-time basis until I know what I want to do in this new life of mine."

"Perfect. You can start tomorrow. I know you will just love all the festivities today has to offer. Go enjoy them. And make sure you try the food Jacob makes. His sandwich shop is to die for."

I gave her a hug and then decided it was time to go see Jacob. Maybe this wouldn't be the worst kind of slavery after all.

~

Jacob—E. Dalia Street

I SAW THAT PATTY HAD found a new friend in Willa and decided I didn't need to keep an eye on her. I focused my attention on making my booth for the restaurant. Sharon had set up the tent and tables last night, so all I I had to do was organize the food and hang the decorations..

"Your booth is looking great, Jacob!" I heard someone say from behind me.

When I turned around, I saw the mayor grinning back at me. "Glad to hear you approve, Mayor Thompson."

"I just knew I could count on you. And I see you brought

a mascot too! I'm sure the big guy is loving this disobedience," Mayor Thompson laughed.

Looking over my right shoulder, I saw Patty walking up to me. She was looking sexy in her outfit all covered in green pixy dust. I watched as it flaked off her skin every time she walked.

"Hi Jacob, can we talk?"

"Mayor, when a pretty woman like this wants my attention, who am I to keep her waiting?"

"Right you are, old man, right you are. Thanks for doing all this. I'll see you two later."

"Thanks for getting me out of that," I said to Patty before turning back towards the decorations.

"No, Jacob," she paused. "I really need to talk to you."

"Oh, okay." I put down what I was holding, pulled out one of the chairs for Patty, and signaled her to sit.

"I don't think I want to work with you."

"Okay, that's fine. We can find something else for you. I know you can be happy here."

She put her hand up to stop me from talking. "I already found a job."

I grinned. "At the bookstore, by chance?"

"How did you know? Did you tell her to come talk to me?"

I held my hands up and shook my head. "No, no, of course not! I just saw you two talking, and I know Willa. You will love her and Raven."

"Oh," Patty said with a sigh. "I think I will, too. I'm going to start tomorrow."

"So that means you agree to stay?"

"Do I really have a choice?"

I slowly shook my head. "Not really. I did trap you."

Patty nodded her head. "That's what I thought. I wanted to discuss my freedom."

"It's done. You're stuck with me." I looked at her pointedly.

"I mean, I want to discuss my freedom in your house. The ability for me to come and go."

"Oh, okay, we can discuss that." I reached my hand out to her, and when she placed her palm in mine, I felt a jolt of electricity soar through my veins.

"That was weird," Patty said.

"You felt that too?" I asked.

Patty grinned. "Yeah, I did."

"I'd like a partner in this. Someone who would help keep my powers charged, but not someone who is a slave to my every need." I watched as Patty thought about what I was saying. "We can make this work. I know it."

When Patty started nodding her head, my spirits lifted, and I thought *this may really work*.

"Can we play things by ear?"

I grinned. "Yes, yes we can."

EPILOGUE

Patty — Jacob's Home — Shifter Lane

When we got home from the day's activities, I couldn't believe I had so much fun celebrating a tradition that my species has been part of in theory but never in reality.

"Did you have fun today?" Jacob asked as he sat on the couch in the living room.

I couldn't stop grinning. "I really did. Everyone was just so great."

"Glad to hear you say that."

"Is everyone always this nice in Hemlock Valley?"

Jacob laughed. "You haven't met the Karens of this town. But yes, overall, the activities are always like this."

"I think I will look forward to getting to know those Karens."

"You say that now, but you don't know how annoying they can be." Jacob laughed again.

"I thought you were supposed to be convincing me to stay?"

"You're staying." He made the statement with a lot of confidence.

"Jury is still out on that."

Jacob lifted his hand and wiggled his finger at me. "Why don't you come join me right here," and he patted his lap.

I sauntered over to him and sat down on his lap. Things throughout the day had been tense, and I wanted to give him a little intimacy. With little thought, I leaned over and kissed him. It wasn't filled with the passion like the sex had been earlier. This was sweet and tender.

Jacob brought his hand up to my cheek and started caressing my skin with his thumb. "I told you that you're going to stay." His hand slipped around behind my head, and he pulled me down towards him, kissing him again.

My body responded to him in such a ferocious way that I knew I would never get tired of that feeling. "You're right. I'm going to stay."

I rested my head on his shoulder, felt his arms wrap around me and hold me close. His fingers danced along my skin, and I could feel my core growing moist.

"Can you feel your powers still growing?" I asked him.

"Mhm," he murmured, "but right now, I just want to focus on this moment and nothing else." Jacob brought his hand to my cheek, turned my face, and captured my lips in a passionate kiss.

"Do you want to see your new room?"

"I hope it's the one with the red comforter." I winked at him.

Jacob laughed, "I had hoped you would say that."

As he lifted me in his arms and started carrying me to our room, I stopped thinking about the what if's of the bad and started focusing on my new future in a demon family.

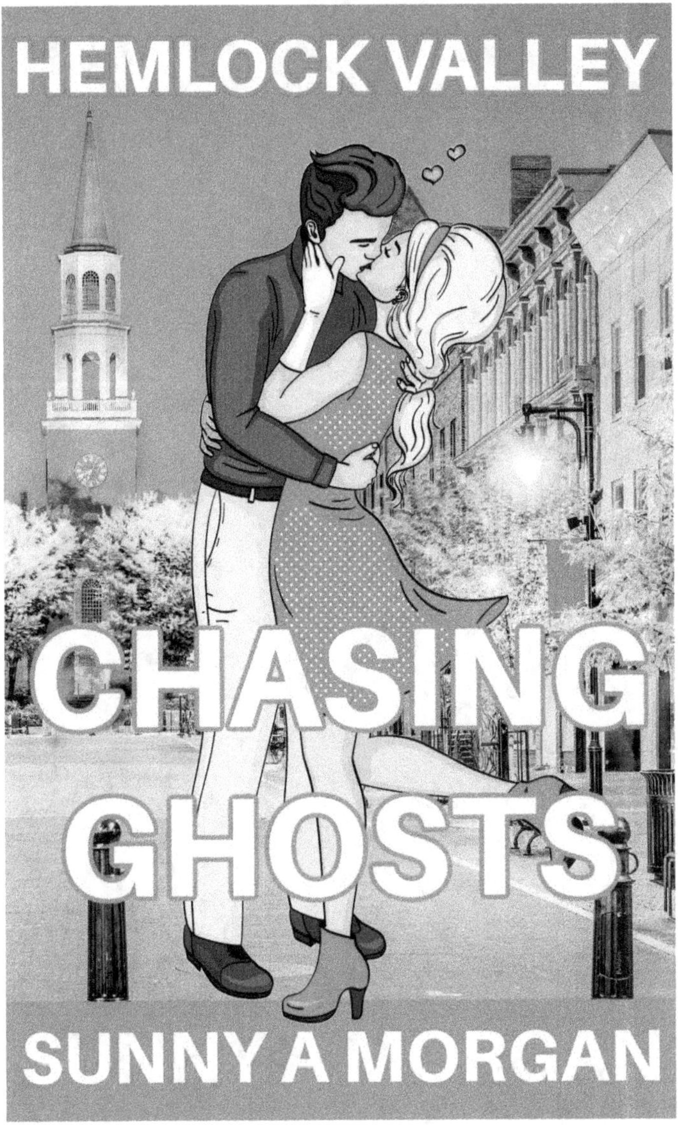
HEMLOCK VALLEY
CHASING GHOSTS
SUNNY A MORGAN

PREFACE

JASON MIDDLETON

I roamed my Queen Anne Victorian style home I had built for her. Around the large fireplace in the main parlor, I admired the elaborate woodwork. I smiled as I walked out onto the massive wrap-around porch. This was Sarah's favorite place to sit and sip her morning tea. She would sit for hours watching the bees fly from one flower to the next. The squirrels yapping at each other as they chased each other from one tree to the next. The sound of the morning birds singing always made her smile. Even in the end, when everything hurt my sweet Sarah, the birds made her smile.

As the years dragged on, many things were lost to me, but my sweet Sarah's smile was not forgotten. My parents' faces disappeared from my memory. My true age was lost to me. Memory after memory faded from my mind over the years. Slowly slipping away like fog through my fingertips. There were times I had to struggle to remember my name. Jason. Jason Middleton. I repeated my name over and over again.

Only a couple of memories remain with me now. One memory that shined for me was the way she looked when the sun filtered through the windows. The way her face would break into a smile when she would catch me watching her.

The other memory was the night she had died. It was burned into my soul. I promised her then I would follow her. I would find her in the afterlife.

She smiled and shook her head. "No, my love. I'll find you in the next life. Look for me."

Then she was gone. My grief led to my early demise through alcohol abuse. I failed the one thing she asked of me. I didn't wait for her to return. Or maybe I am still waiting. I'm trapped in our old home. My Sarah has never returned, and I am stuck here waiting.

People came and went from our home. Most left quickly when I made my presence known. Eventually our home had gained a frightful reputation for being haunted by a strange, sad eyed man.

It had been a long time since anyone had moved into the place, and it was beginning to fall into disrepair. I looked out over the dark grounds that once were full of color.

"Sarah, I've waited for half a century for you to return. You promised you'd come to me." I muttered to myself and closed my eyes.

CHAPTER 1

SARAH

I looked up at the rundown Victorian home and asked myself again why I bought this house. But something drew me to this place, this area. I remembered my grandmother talking about Hemlock Valley when I was a child. She made me promise I would bring her ashes here when she passed.

I stared at the old wrought-iron fence that had seen better days. The lawn needed serious care, and the driveway was covered with debris. Not exactly like the pictures. Hopefully, the house was in better condition.

I left my car parked at the end of the long driveway until I could clear all the debris. With my overnight bag in hand, I walked to the house. I got a funny feeling as I continued closer to the house. It almost felt as if someone was watching me.

"Just the weather and the folklore surrounding Hemlock Valley." I muttered to myself.

Shaking off my nerves, I stepped up onto the porch and

fumbled through my pockets for the keys. When I found the key and put it in the door, it opened by itself before I could turn it.

"I'm not going to die. The realtor probably forgot to lock up." I whispered, trying to convince myself not to run in the opposite direction of this old house.

Slowly, I moved into my new home. I gasped as I looked around. The pictures did not do it justice. Even with a layer of dust, the details were not hidden. I hadn't come to see the home before I purchased it, not my smartest decision, but I fell in love with the traditional Queen Anne Victorian style manor just from the photos. Somehow it felt right to use the money I inherited from my grandmother to buy a home in the place she always spoke so highly of.

I took in my surroundings, dropping my bag at the door as I went into the room to the right. A sitting room, I guessed. White sheets covered the furniture, wallpaper was peeling, and plaster hung from the ceiling.

More work than I expected, but maybe I can find some cheap workers in town.

Lifting the sheets, I peeked underneath to examine the treasures below. "I should probably clean the bedroom and bathroom first." I muttered to myself.

A plan calculating in my head. I grabbed her overnight bag and started up the grand staircase. "Good thing I threw some cleaning supplies in my bag."

I talked to myself a lot as a child, and I continued the habit as an adult. Most of the time, I didn't notice I was doing it until someone pointed it out to me.

After hours of clearing the driveway, unpacking my car, and cleaning, I finally finished the primary bedroom and the adjoining bathroom. The two rooms were exquisite, rundown, but the wood details and the furniture were right out of Gone with the Wind.

I sprayed the mattress with Lysol, doubled up on clean

sheets until I can go to town and buy a new mattress tomorrow. The bathroom was spotless and the oversized clawfoot tub was calling my name.

~

JASON

I TRAILED HER UNSEEN THROUGH my home. Something about her called to me. I felt more—felt something. I couldn't put into words what I felt with her here, but I felt more than loneliness.

Was it hope? Did she bring me hope?

Something in me stirred from her presence. From the moment she stepped through the door, I felt drawn to her in a way that I hadn't felt since…. My Sarah. It can't be, I tell myself as I reached out toward her, only to have a ghostly hand pass through her body. My Sarah did not live, but when I stepped closer, my soul thrummed like a marching band.

"Please see me," I pleaded.

I had never tried to reveal myself before. Driven by an unknown force, I attempted something despite my uncertainty, because I had to know. I followed her as she cleaned, hoping she would see me.

She talked to herself a lot, and it was adorable. As she ran a bath, I watched as pulled her hair up into a bun on top her head. Steam filled the room, and I continued to linger. I should give her privacy, but something made me stay. I needed to see if she had it.

As the tub filled and the room gathered a heavier layer of steam, the grandfather clock chimed loudly, echoing through the halls. Her head snapped toward the door. Reaching, I tried to touch her shoulder, but my fingers slipped through.

Repeatedly, I attempted to muster the energy to show myself, yet nothing happened. I was drained now. Why did I not perfect this when I was stronger? Because there was no reason. No one who called to my soul like this woman. No one tempted me to reveal myself. Until now.

I watched her as she slept. Her graceful lines captivated me. I could see the lines of her as she slept under the light sheet. Underneath, I knew she wore only a nightshirt. I knew because I had watched her change for bed. I felt a bit like a peeping tom watching be I couldn't have been drug away by wild hell hounds. She was stunning. Now here I was, following her like a lost puppy as I watched her as she talked to herself in a way I found entirely too charming.

CHAPTER 2

SARAH

I woke up early the next morning after a fitful sleep. I stretched my tired body as I looked around the room. "Nope, not a dream. It still looks like it came from another era." I muttered as I kicked the blanket from my body.

"Quick shower and off to town." I continued to talk to myself as I gathered a pair of yoga pants and a T-shirt.

"So, I need a new mattress, cause that one is older than my grandmother." I shook in disgust. "Linens, towels, drapes, tons of cleaning supplies." Tapping my chin.

"What else?" I dropped my clothes on the vanity in the bathroom, shrugged off my nightshirt, and turned on the shower. "Hmm, wonder if they updated the plumbing? I'll add that to the list of things to check on. Plumbing, electrical, and the roof. Add those all to my long list of cosmetic DYI projects." Jumping in the warm shower, I quickly cleaned myself as the growing list of to be fixed went through my mind.

"Food, before shopping." I turned to look behind me. I could have sworn I was being followed in the house. Something made me feel like I was being watched.

"Ok boogeyman, come on out so I can see you. If you insist on being here, at least let me see you." I tapped my foot impatiently, waiting for something. I wasn't sure what I was waiting for, but I refused to be afraid. "No? Not going to make yourself known? Are you afraid of a girl?" I snorted a chuckle before running from the house to my car.

Once I arrived in town, I headed straight for the first restaurant; I saw. A small diner called Cherrie's. It looked clean, and the food smelled great.

A short plump lady with large glasses, with the brightest blue eyes and white curly hair, stepped from the back.

"Whatcha want, honey? A table or counter?" The southern drawl snapped me to attention. Unusual for this far north.

"Yes, ma'am." I replied.

"Yes, to what, child? Table or counter? You don't look slow, are you slow, girl?" The woman smirked.

"Oh, sorry counter, ma'am." I whispered as I headed for the counter, following the wobbly waitress.

"No need to be sorry, honey. And the names Cherrie. You're new to these parts, aren't ya?"

"Yes, mam—I mean Cherrie. I just bought the old manor off the main road about five miles south." I replied, sipping the coffee.

The gasp that came from Cherrie filled the diner. "Girl, you best get your skinny behind out of that house. Before the Middleton ghost gets you."

"Middleton ghost?" I asked. "Cherrie, I don't believe in ghosts." With a fake confidence, I added. I had felt something in that house from the moment I stepped in the door, but I wasn't going to let it run me off.

"Girly, you best start believing in ghosts because whether

or not you believe, there is something not right about that house. Sarah Middleton died fifty years ago in childbirth and her husband Jason died a few years later died from a broken heart. It is said he still walks the halls of his home, waiting for Sarah to return." Cherrie said.

"Sarah? His wife's name was Sarah?" I stuttered.

Cherrie leaned across the counter and lowered her voice. "Yes. Her last words to Jason were: *I'll find you in the next life. Look for me.*"

"My name is Sarah." I muttered.

Cherrie's eyes went wide before she stood up straight. "Oh, honey, lots of women are named Sarah."

"Yeah." I said.

My mind was racing now. What if this ghost thinks I'm his wife? "Don't be stupid, there is no ghost." I mumbled to myself.

I finished up my coffee and asked. "Can you make a turkey sandwich to go? I think I want to shop right away. A lot to buy to get my house livable again."

"Sure thing, honey, but the best thing you could do was to move on out of there." Shaking her head, Cherrie went to the kitchen.

My fingers tapped against the counter while I waited for the feisty waitress to bring my lunch. I turned, looking over my shoulder. I couldn't shake the feeling like someone was watching me. Shrugging, I grabbed a napkin and a pen from the counter and started making a list, whispering to myself as I did. "Linens, more cleaning supplies, toiletries, a few groceries... what else" I sighed. "Come on, Sarah, what else do you need? A mattress."

"Honey, who are you talking to?" Cherrie asked as she barreled through the swinging door leading from the kitchen. "Child, are you talking to yourself?"

I started to red, embarrassed. I was caught. "Umm, yes

ma'am, I was just writing my list of things I'll need from town." I held up the napkin, stumbling over my words.

"No need to explain. I just wanted to be sure you didn't bring that ghost with you." Cherrie handed me a bag. "It's Cherrie remember girly. Now when you go to Stew's hardware, tell him Cherrie sent you and he will help you find someone crazy enough to work at the Middleton house."

Laughing, I grabbed the bag and thanked Cherrie for her time. I headed out, but turned around quickly. "I almost forgot to pay. How much?"

Waving her hand at me. "First meal is always free honey, gotta get you Yankees hooked on my food, then I'll charge ya'll double." She laughed, and her belly moved with her laughter.

"I'll see you soon and thanks so much for everything." I smiled, waving as I left the diner.

CHAPTER 3

JASON

*W*hen she left the house, I trailed behind her, and it was as though she was a magnet. Pulling me from the house to her. She drove to a diner and sat down, conversing with a serving woman as I watched with rapt attention, trying not to be awed with my surroundings.

I followed her from the diner, feeling lost and confused. This modern world was frightening and new. Entering shops behind her, I observed her effortlessly chatting with the shopkeepers. I walked behind her as she wandered aisle after aisle of household items and moved on to furniture. I was pleased when she stopped at the *As The Emerald Turns Bookstore*. My Sarah and I loved this shop.

"Hello, my name is Willa and if I can help you find anything, please let me know." The pretty young woman said.

"Hi, I'm Sarah. It's nice to meet you. This place is amazing." Sarah gushed.

"Thank you. It's been in the family for generations." Willa said.

I watched as Sarah wandered the aisles of books. She periodically touched books she felt drawn to.

"Jason. I know you're here." Willa whispered behind me.

I gasped, and Willa chuckled. I tried speaking, but nothing was audible.

"It's a gift. No one else can see you. Yet." Willa looked over her shoulder at Sarah. "But she will, soon."

Before I could try to speak, Willa dashed off to help another customer.

"Thank you. I'll be back soon." Sarah said before she left the bookstore empty handed.

I felt dazed when we finally returned home and that strange world was locked away again. I watched as she unpacked her car and set to work. She cleaned and scrubbed the bathroom, the kitchen, and she worked until she the entire house was spotless. She had to be exhausted, but you couldn't tell by the way she was bouncing with excitement when the delivery men brought her new mattress.

I had to admit; she had a nice ass. While she was making her new bed, I couldn't help but admire it. I was tempted to pat her backside, but I stopped myself. I probably wouldn't be able to do it anyway and it was rude. But it was tempting.

CHAPTER 4

IT'S ALL A DREAM

SARAH

I turned the corner and entered a garden. Clusters of trees, flowering vines, and gorgeous fountains stood on the lush grounds. Reds, oranges, greens in various shades, and the exotic, sweet perfume of the flowers surrounded me. The delicate sounds of stringed instruments floated in the air. I followed a path up a shallow flight of stairs. Everything around me was magical. There was a lovely pool in the middle of this outdoor room. The terrace was gorgeous, with interlocking mosaic tiles placed in a complicated pattern. Off to the side was an enormous bed centered on a wooden platform. It was covered in silk and piled high with pillows in every shade of the sunset. On a low table there was a burner filled with incense that smelled of sex and wicked desires.

I whispered. "This is lovely."

"I'm glad you like it." A male's voice filled the outdoor room. He stood on the other side of the terrace, behind a curtain.

I tucked a curling strand of hair behind my ear. Slowly, I walked to meet the voice. I pulled the curtain aside and stepped through. The sun was softer here, filtered by colorful sheer curtains swaying at the corners of the veranda. The sun peeked through the material, casting shadows of red and gold. At first, all I noticed was the male's silhouette. The sun shining through the curtains played over his skin. I tucked a strand of my hair behind one ear. I walked slowly to meet the stranger. Deep inside, I knew this was all a dream, but I still felt nervous. I pulled a curtain aside and stepped through. The sun was softer here, filtered by silk drapes fluttering at the edges of the terrace. The sun peeked through the silk, casting shadows of red and gold. At first, all she could see was his silhouette against the sun, the colors of the silk playing over his skin. He was shirtless, and I could make out the rounded curve of wide shoulders, strong, muscular arms. I swallowed hard. I felt like a schoolgirl.

"Sarah" A deep voice, edged with a soft husky tone, that was familiar.

I took another step forward, and the glare of the sun moved into shadow, revealing him to me. Thick dark hair framed a face that was all chiseled planes, softened by the lush curve of his mouth. When he smiled at me, his eyes were dark, nearly black. Skin the color of dark honey, and so smooth. He rose to his feet, every motion graceful, and towered over me. I felt small, delicate in his presence.

He moved toward me, one hand outstretched. "Come, Sarah"

My throat was suddenly dry. He was so beautiful and at this moment I could not breathe from the intensiveness of his gaze. He was the most spectacularly intimidating man I had set eyes on. My skin tingled simply looking at him.

His smile made me light-headed as my blood rushed through my veins. I had to look beyond him for a moment, to the view of the rugged, dusky gray mountains against the backdrop of bright blue sky. My breath went right out of me when he touched my hand. Like fire. Like electricity on my skin. Was it only my nerves that made me react like this?

"Come and sit by the water with me." His fingers folded around mine and my skin went hot beneath his touch as I followed him across the terrace.

I couldn't speak, could barely think. I'd never been so stunned by the mere presence of another person in my life. Calm down. He led me to the edge of the marble pool. There were handfuls of flower petals that danced as the water moved. Then his hand was on my chin, lifting my face so I was forced to look into those glittering black eyes.

"Don't look away, Sarah. I want to see you. And you need to see me, to know me. I've waited so long for you to return. You mustn't be afraid."

Blinking, I looked up at him. "I'm not afraid. I'm just confused. I know you, but I don't."

He smiled, the corners of that lush mouth lifting a little. His mouth was too beautiful when he smiled. And I was going to touch it, to kiss him. I needed to calm myself, to let go of my fear, my tension, if I was going to enjoy this. It was just a dream, after all. And he was far too good not to enjoy. I pushed away any doubts he did not find me sexy enough.

"You're thinking too much. I can feel it." He lifted his hand to touch my cheek.

"Yes." Heat crept into my cheeks.

"I believe I may have the perfect cure for that." He moved around behind me, slid his hands over my shoulders.

He was so close I could feel the heat of him against my back. When he leaned in, his breath was warm in my hair.

His voice was low, soft. "Give yourself over to me, Sarah. To me. I will take care of your every need, I promise you."

A shiver ran through me, making gooseflesh rise on my skin.

He went on. "You must learn to relax. To let go all of

those thoughts running through your mind, holding you back from the pleasure of the moment. I'll help you."

His hands slid down my bare arms. His touch was warm, reassuring, and sparking fires of need everywhere he touched that reached down deep in my belly. "Will you allow me to do this for you, Sarah?"

Right now, I wanted to allow him to do anything. I was safe, after all. This was only a dream. This beautiful stranger could do anything to me. My stranger. Even as my pulse hammered with fear, the word came out in a whisper. "Yes."

"Ah, I knew you could do it." His hands moved back up, and his fingers threaded through my hair. "Such glorious hair," he said. "Like satin. And the sun lights it up in red and gold."

Another long shiver went through my system. I could not believe this was really happening. He went on, his voice that same low, soothing murmur. "I want you to become comfortable with me. Do you like the water, Sarah?"

"Yes. I love the water."

"Then swim with me."

I nodded. "Just let me get a suit."

"There's no need. It's only the two of us here." He moved away from me, and I turned just in time to see him untie the strings on his loose linen pants. "My stranger, my ghost." Even as my pulse hammered with fear, the word came out in a whisper.

He led me by the hand, guiding me into the water. The lotus flowers floating in the water parted as we went deeper into the pool. The temperature was perfect, warm enough to be soothing and comfortable. It felt surreal, strange, and wonderful to be here at this moment with this beautiful man. We watched one another as we floated. So many thoughts ran through my head. I wanted him. It surprised me at how much I wanted him. However, every muscle in my body craved him. Jason took my hand from under the water, raising it to his lips. His wet lips were cool and soft. They moved to my fingers; he kissed each one. Making my body ache.

"Tell me when to stop and I will. Tell me what you want, and it will be yours. Do you understand, my sweet Sarah?"

"I — I understand. I think, but I honestly do not know what I want," I confessed.

"I know you are nervous, especially now that you know recognize me, but you do not need to be. Everything that will happen in this dream in this moment will only happen if you will it." Jason silently moved in behind me. "I would like to touch you. May I touch you?"

I breathed out slowly before I could think about it, "Yes." This simple word I said to this man repeatedly. Yes.

"Lean into me, Sarah. I will do it all. Let me?" Jason pressed his body into my back. "I've dreamed of being with you again for decades." He breathed in my ear. "Finally, you're here with me again. I almost lost hope."

His arms wrapped around my mid-section, and I fell limp against him. Jason held me to his body. "Trust me and let me take care of your needs."

"I want to, I'm trying to," I mumbled. "It feels too real, not like the dreams before."

"Because you've returned to me," Jason whispered in my ear. "I want to touch you, to feel your nether lips open for me. Will you allow me to touch you more?"

"Yes." The simple word slipped from my lips.

He moved like the water, graceful, fluidly. The heat from his body warmed me. He was so strong and large, but his hands slid over my body smoothly, softly, almost like a whisper of a touch. My stomach muscled clenched when his large palm touched me. His hand smoothed over the curve of my hip. I felt myself come alive under his hands.

My sex wanted and tightened with desire, lust, need. I fixated on the hard mass of his powerful chest behind me, the heavy bulge of his cock unyielding against my back. When he slipped his fingertips over my breasts, a small gasp slipped from me.

"Let it happen," he crooned. "It's just us." Jason's fingers traced the stiff buds of my nipples. "Allow me the honor of pleasuring you again. I've missed you for so long."

"Yes…" Did I know any other words? I refused to question myself now. This experience is what I wanted. I needed this experience. My body was begging for him.

Jason's powerful hands cupped my breasts, and the water flowing around me felt incredible.

Desire flowed over my body. I fixed my gaze back on the mountains in the distance while he kneaded and squeezed my flesh. I had to fight the urge not to press my body into him more. One of his hands' fingers rolled over my nipples while the other slid down my belly.

He hesitated. "Tell me you want this, my sweet Sarah."

My pussy clenched, went hot, and drenched with need. I decided at that moment to give myself over to him, to this experience. "I do. Please touch Jason."

"With pleasure, your every desire is my command." Jason moved his hand to my core. His finger slipped through my folds.

Ecstasy pushed through me, bringing the need for release quickly. His fingers continued to play over my body, causing me to pant. "Jason," I moaned.

"You need it quickly. This release is needed badly, but next time I will take my time. I will tease you for hours before allowing you to cum. But this time it must be swift." Jason pressed two thick fingers deep inside my sex.

I moaned as he fucked his fingers in and out of my pussy. Pleasure piercing through my body.

He used his thumb to steadily circle my clit. I could not suppress my moans or my body shaking. "Ah, very good, my sweet Sarah." His warm breath tickled my ear.

His thumb pressed harder, and his fingers thrusted faster.

"Oh!" The shot of pleasure was shocking; it was that intense, that deep. My first wave of my orgasm rushed through me. "Please," I cried.

"My pleasure." His hand moved faster; fingers buried inside of my pussy.

I came in an overwhelming surge, the tormenting ache of lust sated. The water danced around us. It was almost sensual how it moved against our naked bodies.

When I finally stopped trembling, Jason turned me in his arms. My head fell instantly to his chest. Humility washed over me at this moment. I felt grateful. I still wanted him and needed him inside of me.

"Make love to me." I whispered.

I woke up gasping for air; my hand went to my chest as my eyes flew open. Looking around frantically, I realized I was in my bedroom alone. The dream was so real. One moment I was wandering a beautiful garden and the next I was asking who I assumed was Jason Middleton to make love to me. I closed my eyes; the memories of the dream flooded me, suffocating. Fear slammed into me, the emotion beating in my head. I saw it all so clearly in my mind. The dream returned. I used to have that same dream for years. But now it felt more real. Jason. I had a name for my dream lover.

I shook my head. "It was only a dream and my imagination running away with me. There is no way the man in my dreams was Jason Middleton."

CHAPTER 5

JASON

I know it was wrong, but I entered her dream. It was a terrible idea to guide her mind during such a vulnerable time, but I needed to see if it was my Sarah. If my Sarah finally returned to me. She did return. It's her. I'm not sure how reincarnation works, but this woman is my wife. It was necessary for me to find a way to get her to see it herself.

I looked around the house as Sarah unpacked and hung pictures. She continued to talk to herself and occasionally I caught her smiling. Her smile was contagious.

The door bell rung and Sarah rushed to the door. "Hi, do you remember me? We met at my bookstore." Willa said as she shuffled a large bag from one arm to the next.

"Yes, Willa. Please come in." Sarah offered.

"I'm sorry to just barge in on you like this, but I brought some things I think you need to see," Willa said.

"Umm, okay." Sarah said skeptically. "We can sit at the dining table."

Willa followed Sarah into the dining room and laid her

overstuffed bag on top. "I'm not sure if you believe in the paranormal, like ghosts and reincarnation or not, but living in Hemlock Valley, you are going to get your fill of paranormal experiences."

"I read a lot about Hemlock Valley and my grandmother told me about the folklore surrounding the town." Sarah said, as she took a seat across from Willa.

"You see, folklore is not just stories here. It's our history. We have vampires, shifters, goblins, and ghosts just to name a few supernatural beings that reside in our quaint little town. Ghosts is my main reason for my visit." Willa said.

Willa pulled out several photos and handed one to Sarah. "This is the couple who built this house. Sarah and Jason Middleton. She looks a lot like you."

Sarah examined the picture, and I looked over her shoulder. I remember that day it was taken. The day before she died. Sarah looked beautiful, her belly round with our baby. If I could cry, I would.

"We look a little alike." Sarah said softly.

"There is a legend about the couple. Just before Sarah died in childbirth, she promised Jason she would return and for him to wait for her here. In this house." Willa said, pulling another picture out of Sarah and me and pushed it across the table.

"That's a romantic story, but just a fairytale." Sarah said, pushing the photos back toward Willa.

"I saw Jason following you at my bookstore." The words burst out of Willa in an excited breath.

"What?" Sarah exclaimed.

"He's here now. Aren't you Jason?" Willa asked, looking directly at me.

Could she really see me? To finally have someone acknowledge my existence felt unreal.

"Are you saying you see him now?" Sarah asked, looking around the room.

"He is right behind you." Willa answered.

Sarah frantically looked behind her and around the room. I tried to will myself visible, but I just wasn't strong enough.

"You're kidding. Is this like some welcome to Hemlock Valley hazing?" Sarah laughed nervously.

"I know this is unbelievable and kinda scary, but it's true I see him behind you." Willa said.

"Okay, let's say there is a ghost living in my house. What can I do about it?" Sarah asked.

"He isn't going to harm you. He believes you're his wife, finally returning to him." Willa added. "I think he might be right."

"YES!" I shouted, to no avail. Neither Sarah nor Willa acknowledged the sound.

"That's not possible." Sarah said.

"Oh, but it is. I think I can bring him forward if you would like to talk to him." Willa suggested.

"What?" Sarah Asked.

CHAPTER 6

SARAH

This was not happening. But it felt kind of real, and a weird part of me wanted to be Sarah Middleton.

"What would you do to bring him forward? Would it prove I was Sarah Middleton in a past life?" I asked.

Just asking those questions felt ridiculous.

"Honestly, I'm not sure if it will prove if you were Sarah in a past life, but I am pretty sure I can help Jason come forward and talk to us," Willa explained. "With a séance."

I took a deep breath and looked around the room. "Okay, let's do this."

Willa clapped her hands. "Yay!" She exclaimed as she started unpacking her bag. "Let's get started."

"What now? Doesn't it have to be dark?" I asked.

Willa laughed. "It's not a movie. We can do this any time of day. But you will need to shut all the drapes and lower the lights."

"Umm, okay." I said as I got up to close the curtains.

Willa gave me instructions on how to ready the area for

the séance. We worked in silence, laying out rocks, lighting the numerous brass candelabras and the dozen tea light candles surrounding the room, placing various herbs and crystals in a circle.

We sat at the dining table. Willa took the pictures of the Middletons and placed them carefully in the center of the table. She laid a few stones from her velvet pouch around the pictures.

I was surprised to feel the power already. It was both comforting and alarming. Willa's dramatic tone drew my attention from my thoughts. She called to the earth, wind, water, and fire as she knitted her magic that hung over the room like a shimmering net. She led us in a series of chants before she started to call for Jason to show himself.

We waited expectantly for a few moments, but nothing happened. "It didn't work," I said.

"Hush." Willa said. "Jason, show yourself."

I rolled my eyes as Willa's voice took a lower, more ominous tone. "We demand your presence."

"Demand?" I questioned in a whispered tone.

"We are here to help you. Let us see you. We want to find a way to set you free." Willa continued.

The flames from the candles began to crackle and dance around the room. I drew in a short breath and shivered at the sudden cold that encumbered the area. He was here. At least I hoped it was him and not something else.

A ghostly form began to take shape, hovering a foot above the wood floor. "Can you really see me?" A shaky voice asked.

"Shit," I muttered in disbelief. I felt Willa squeeze my hand tighter.

"Yes, Jason. I can see and hear you," Willa answered.

"I can not believe it after decades of waiting for you, Sarah. You are finally here." The ghost said.

"Why do you think I'm your dead wife?" I asked quietly.

"I just know." Jason replied.

"But how? I'm only thirty years old. Your wife died fifty years ago." I asked.

"Willa can probably explain it better than me, but I just know. I knew the moment you walked into the house. You finally came back to me," Jason said. His image was becoming clearer.

"Maybe the séance was not a good idea," I whispered.

"Why did you decide to move here?" Jason asked.

I took a deep breath. "I'm dying. I have ovarian cancer and I'm in the last stage of my life. I was drawn here. My grandmother always told me about this place, and I wanted to finally do something adventurous. Moving to a new place where no one knows I'm sick and just living life for the time I have left."

"You came to be with me," Jason said.

"I think he's right." Willa added.

"Let's say I am Sarah Middleton and I found my way back here. How would it work? When I die, how do we know I'll end up with Jason?" I asked.

This all seemed so unreal, but part of me knew they were right. I have a past life, and this ghost was part of that life.

"Willa, is there something we can do to help my communication with Sarah?" Jason asked.

"I have something better." Willa said, holding up a little bottle. "If Sarah drinks this when she is ready to know the truth, I can guarantee you two will be together when her time comes."

"Really?" Both Jason and I asked at the same time.

"Yes. Don't ask how it works. Just trust my madness." Willa laughed. "Don't be nervous. It's a little magical potion. Just call me Pheobe."

"Who?" Jason asked.

"It's a witch from a TV show." I said.

"Maybe I should go and let you process everything." She added as she gathered her belongings.

"Wait. What about him?" I asked, waving my hand toward the ghostly figure.

"He'll be around for a bit from my magic. It will wear off in a few hours, but he could stick around longer." Willa shrugged. "Maybe if you two get to know each other a little more, memories of your past together will come forward, Sarah."

Willa dashed out the door, leaving me standing in my dining room with a ghost who is supposedly my husband from fifty years ago. This all seemed normal.

"Tell me about your life with Sarah." I finally said as I walked into the main living room.

Jason followed me and took a seat. Well, he sort of took a seat in the wingback chair next to mine. He kind of hovered over the chair.

"We moved here before the transition of Hemlock Valley into a paranormal tourist site. Sarah loved the Victorian style homes, and we both fell in love with this land. We had the house built in the style of Queen Anne Victorian homes of the early 1900s. We would dance under the stars, swim naked in our marble pool, make love in every room of the house." Jason said with longing.

"That sounds lovely." I said as visions of Jason and Sarah dancing filled her head.

The resemblance was uncanny. My resemblance to his wife made reincarnation feel possible in that moment.

"I've felt stronger since you've been here. I am almost completely solid right now," Jason added, as he looked at his arms.

"What if, when I die, I don't stay with you?" I asked.

"You are so comfortable with your death. How is that possible?" Jason asked.

I was quiet for several moments before I answered. "I

have a few months, maybe longer, but I am ready. My last few months shouldn't be filled with worry about my approaching end. I want to live while I am here, and I want to die on my terms. Which means not being afraid."

"Very brave." He looked at me with such longing, it was heartbreaking.

"Not really." I said as I stood. "I'm going to take a nap."

I was getting tired, and I needed a break from the entire reincarnation idea.

"Of course, I'll be here." He sounded disappointed.

CHAPTER 7

SARAH

I stepped into my bedroom and changed into a T-shirt. My brain was exhausted and my body hurt. A long nap was what I needed.

I always loved our library, especially the poetry section. I fingered a copy of E. E. Cummings before flipping to one of my favorite poems.

Lady, I Will Touch You

I gasped when I felt strange fingers brush my thigh and grasp the hem of my dress. "Sarah." Jason breathed as I leaned back into him. "Hold up the book, Sarah. Let me read the poem to you."

My heart began to beat faster, his hot breath against my neck, and his obvious erection pressed into my back. I opened the book wide to give him the best view possible.

Lady, I will touch you with my mind.

Touch you and touch and touch until you give me

His fingers trailed up my thighs, moving further with each word he read.

Suddenly a smile, shyly obscene
Lady, I will touch you with my mind
Touch you, that is all,

I moaned at the first touch of his finger, slipping through my panties and touching my wet pussy lips.

Lightly and you utterly will become
With infinite care
The poem which I do not write

His finger sliding in and out of my pussy made it hard to focus on his words.

"How does it feel, sweetheart?"

"Whaa —" I trailed off.

"How does it feel to know I can give you what you crave? That I'm going to fuck your tight pussy until you're a whimpering mess." His deep voice growled in my ear.

His fingers continued to work my pussy, curling inside, hitting my g-spot. His free hand fisted inside my hair and turned my head. His mouth took mine in a hard kiss, swallowing my cries. His finger worked faster, coaxing my orgasm to the forefront.

"I need to be inside you."

I moaned, my body pressed against the shelf. "Yes." I panted.

He chuckled when I cried out after he pulled his finger from my pussy. He smacked my ass. "On your knees."

I dropped immediately. My hands fumbled to undo his belt. He pushed my hands away and unbutton his pants and pushed them and his briefs down his legs. I traced the length of his cock with the tip of my nail. It jumped at my touch.

Jason hissed, his fingers threaded through my long hair. He yanked my head back, forcing me to look up at him. "Open your pretty little mouth." He demanded.

Tilting my head back and opening my mouth, his cock head grazed my tongue. I closed my lips around it and sucked gently. I took more of him into my mouth, licking along the underside of his cock. His hips flexed and pushed forward, forcing me to take more. He pulled almost all the way out and thrusted back in a hard.. I couldn't stop the gag that his movement caused, but this seemed to spur him on. His finger dug into my scalp and thrusted his cock to the back of my throat. "Sarah," he hissed. He didn't hold back. He fucked my face without thinking about my comfort. My eyes watered, spit dribbled down my chin, and my scalp stung from his tight grip.

His cock swelled and stretched in my mouth and throat. Jason snarled and pushed me off his cock. He picked me up and pushed me back against the wall. Jason ripped my panties off of me and pulled my loose dress off my body. He roughly massaged my tit before he pushed my lace bra over my breasts. His cock hit my stomach and as his mouth claimed my breast. His tongue swirled around the tip of my nipple before he sucked into his mouth. Lifting my body, his hands went under my arms. My legs went around his waist, his cock impaling my pussy.

"Yes." I moaned.

"You're so fucking tight, sweetheart." He growled. "You feel so good."

It hurt, but it hurt so good.

"This is going to be quick, my sweet Sarah. Are you almost there?" Jason groaned.

"Yes. So close." I panted, squeezing my vaginal muscles around his cock.

He almost pulled out before he rammed back in hard. His thumb went to my clitoris and his teeth sunk into my neck.

I screamed. "JASON."

"Fuck Sarah." He moaned.

My head fell back, my eyes closed as my orgasm tore through me. He thrusted a few more times and then I felt his cock twitch and his hot seed shoot inside of me.

He buried his face in the curve of my neck and lightly

kissed my skin. Jason slowly lowered me to the ground. "Fuck, my sweet Sarah."

I laughed softly. "Yes, that was intense."

He lifted his head and dropped his forehead to mine. "Are you alright?"

I smiled, "Yes."

He stepped away and helped straightened my bra and dress before he dressed himself. "Remind me to take my lunch breaks from home more often."

I woke up with a smile on my face. This dream did not scare me like the last one. This one felt more like a memory. It felt real.

CHAPTER 8

JASON

I heard Sarah moaning in her sleep; she was dreaming about us. She was dreaming about the time I came home for lunch, and we made love in the library. It was one of my favorite memories as well.

I knew without a doubt she was, in fact, my Sarah and she was starting to believe it too. In just the few days she has been here, I have become stronger.

"You're still visible." Sarah said when she woke from her nap.

"I am." I agreed.

"Have you been watching me sleep?" She asked as she stretched and sat up in her bed.

I shook my head. "No, well, not the entire time. I heard you making noises. I wanted to check and make sure you were alright."

She stared at me for a moment before she nodded. "I can't believe I'm going to say this, but I want to drink the potion."

"Really?" I rushed to her and reached out to touch her cheek.

My hand was solid, and I was able to briefly touch her soft skin before my hand faded.

"Does that mean you believe you are my Sarah?" I asked.

She smiled at me, and I swear it felt like it was fifty years ago. "Yes, it's crazy and makes no sense, but I do. And what's the harm? I'm dying in a few months. What harm will it do for me to believe in a little paranormal magic?"

"I guess you don't have much to lose." I pointed at the small bottle on her bedside table. "Are you going to drink it now?"

Sarah looked over at the bottle, then back at me. "Why wait?" She picked up the bottle, pulled the cork, and downed the liquid in one shot. "Guess it's in the hands of the fates now." She said with a wink.

"I want to hold you so badly." I said.

"If Willa is right, you will get your chance soon enough."

EPILOGUE

SARAH

*I*t's been seven months since I moved to Hemlock Valley and one month since my death. Willa was right. I ended up with Jason. Exactly where I was meant to be. Willa was an important part of our afterlife plan. She helped set up a trust for our home to remain empty but maintained. Luckily, my grandmother was a wealthy woman, and I inherited a lot of money after her death. Willa's best friend Rayven helped set up financial planning to hopefully maintain our house for decades to come.

Jason has gotten stronger. He can make himself solid for a few hours at a time. I can not, but maybe one day.

"Sarah, come play with us," Jason yelled from the garden.

Us. Our daughter is now with us. Our daughter returned to us. She returned as a toddler and neither of us are sure why she was only three physically now or where she has been since my first death. Truthfully, right now we couldn't care less. We are just happy to be together again.

The thing about life is nothing is as simple as black or white. All those other colors slip in and that is where the unexplainable magic happens.

HEMLOCK VALLEY

EASTER BUNNY MADE ME DO IT

SKYLAR QUINN

PREFACE

*O*nce again, the anticipation of the clock winding down to zero had my tail in a flurry of pats. It was the most exciting and annoying day of the year for me. The day I became a human.

The lord and master of my freedom, Jerome, won me in a gambling match in the late 1900s and ever since, I have been trapped like an animal. I understand the irony, seeing as I am currently a rabbit. But it wasn't always like this.

When I first developed my powers back in my small village in Germany, in the late 17th century, everyone thought it was more parlor trick than anything else. Being able to manipulate eggs. One thing led to another and suddenly I was making money, being hired for children's parties. Back then, there wasn't much for entertainment, so I was a bit of a phenomenon. I would travel to different villages with my friends.

It was a good life until we stumbled onto a witch. My boyfriend at the time double crossed her. We didn't know that's what was happening until it was too late. Her name was Hexa Lemp, and she was a vile woman. She raised rabbits to do experiments on them, hoping to perfect her skill to turn to people. My boyfriend Felix was appalled when we discovered this and set out to stop her.

Truthfully, it was so long ago; I don't remember exactly what he had done to get caught. But she killed him right in front of me. Our friends had escaped, but I went back to save him and got caught, too. She decided I would make a great rabbit for an experiment and changed me from a human to an animal.

But when she tried to cast her next curse on me, nothing happened. Nothing ever happened. For eleven months she tried to torment me, but I just sat here, starving for food.

Until one day I woke up and was human again. I thought Hexa grew a conscious, but it turned out Mother Nature had the last laugh. One month a year, I got to be human. There was an invisible tether that kept her, and I bonded. I could never go too far away from her. Until she found a spell to transfer ownership of me.

The last time that spell was used was in 1896 at a tavern in this city. It was the postmaster, Andrew Jackson, who won me, and who keeps me as his pet.

Life has been worse, I have to admit. At least this tormentor feeds me and lets kids play with me. But at some point, I deserve my freedom.

Some of the town people know my story. But I don't think anyone believes me, honestly. It's like they think I am living simply to hide eggs for kids. But there is so much more than that at play going on. I am ready for freedom, and I am ready to take revenge on Andrew Jackson for keeping me tethered to him for so many years.

He told me once he forgot the spell. He probably did. But that doesn't excuse things.

It just makes it that much more complicated.

CHAPTER 1

DAISY - LOCATION: N. LILY STREET

*I*t was the first day of my freedom in Hemlock Valley and I would not waste a moment of it. Of course, I would still lay the eggs for the kids in a few days, but today was all about me. It had been one of the few things I still loved to do. But I was determined this year to break free of the curse.

I watched so many creatures coming in and out of the postmaster's office this year that I realized I needed to find a more powerful wizard. One that I could convince of my plight in life was worthy of a reversal. I wasn't sure how I was going to do it, but I had determination and fortitude. And that's what mattered.

Hemlock Valley hadn't changed a lot in the time I had spent visiting the city once a year. The store fronts all looked the same. Some had updated paint or windows, others had new signage. The feel, atmosphere, and overall essence of this small town never changed year after year. There was something that was comforting about that, truthfully. The fact that there was so much predictability in it should help me in my plans, in theory.

"Well, I guess I know what time of year it is," I heard a deep voice say from behind me.

My spine danced with goosebumps caused by the voice. He always teased me that he was free to run about the town, without consequence, doing as he pleased. Slowly turning around, I plastered a smile on my face.

"Cupid, how lovely to see you!" The smile on my face was fake, and he knew it. Cupid and I had a love hate relationship. We loved to hate each other.

"The pleasure is always all mine, you sexy bunny."

"How many times do I have to tell you I am not a bunny?" I brought my arms up and crossed them over my chest.

"If it looks like a duck, feels like a duck, smells like a duck, guess what? It's a duck."

I let out a deep breath. "Every year I explain to you the witch did this to me. She changed me from a human to an animal. I am a human."

"And every year," he said as he closed the distance between us, "I tell you that you're still the sexiest bunny I know."

"Why do you do this to me? The constant teasing.?"

He shrugged. "Mythological creatures like us have to stick together."

"Stick together means help me break the curse. Not tease me every day, every year, all the time."

"How would you know I cared if I didn't tease?" Cupid was now standing right next to me. I could feel the heat radiating off his skin.

"Stop. If you cared, you would have done something more than this many years ago." I turned around and started to walk away.

"Hey, wait up!" Cupid started walking alongside me. "What are you going to do with your first day of freedom?"

"I'm looking for a wizard."

"Don't you belong to a wizard?"

I snapped my head in his direction, glaring at him. "I don't belong to anyone."

He rested his hand on my arm. "Daisy, stop. You know what I mean."

Shrugging his hand off my arm. "I am looking for someone to help me break the curse. There are so many creatures here. There has to be someone more powerful than Andrew Jackson!"

He nodded his head. "We could go to As The Emerald Turns. Those two ladies know everyone. I'm sure they know a wizard or two."

I shook my head. "Raven tried freeing me last year. We didn't have any success." I almost felt like crying, but I sucked it up. I wouldn't give into anything of those sorts, especially in front of Cupid.

"I'm sorry, Daisy. I know this sucks."

He actually sounded like he cared for me, and I wasn't sure how I felt about that.

"If you have any ideas, you know about powerful wizards. Let me know."

"I will."

My feet started moving again, and before I knew it, I had walked away from Cupid and this time, he hadn't followed me. It was hard seeing him. He had always claimed he was in the town for good, but he didn't know how much I could see from my cell eleven months a year. I saw the humans and creatures falling in love and breaking up. After losing Felix, I hated love. Especially since I couldn't have it ever again.

"Daisy!"

I heard the friendly voice shouting my name and knew instantly who it was.

"Cherrie!" I said in return. We walked towards each other, embracing in a warm hug.

"I'm so glad you're back. We've missed you."

Cherrie Davis was one of the kindest wolf shifters I had met. She always let me eat at her café when I was in human form, even though I never had money.

"Thank you for saying that. I just ran into Cupid, and you know how he teases me."

"That's because he likes you. You know that!"

I sighed, shaking my head and then smiling at her. "It's good to see a friendly face."

"When was your first day back?" she asked.

"Today. Thirty days to figure out how to stay for good."

"Oh, sweetie, you must be starving. Come on, let's get you some food."

She tugged at my arm and started pulling me toward Cherrie's Café, her restaurant. I didn't resist because I was hungry, and I loved her food.

"Will you eat with me?" Catch me up on the town gossip?"

Her hand patted my arm. I could feel her smiling without seeing her face. "Of course! Did you know we now have a leprechaun in town?"

"I did not!"

She nodded. "A demon and a leprechaun, who would have thought?"

"I can't believe it. Which demon?"

"Jacob Martin!"

I let out an honest to god gasp, "No!"

She nodded. "Yes. Can you believe it? Hopefully, you will run into her. She is very sweet."

Jacob Martin was not the man I ever pictured to settle down and take a lover, let alone a mythical creature. "I can't believe Cupid didn't tell me there was another one of us in town now. He always teases, never anything serious."

"Well, she is lovely. I'll introduce you to her. Patty is her name."

We were at the front of her café, and someone opened the

front door for us. We walked inside and she sat me down at a booth.

"Look over the menu, I'll be right back to take your order. On the house, as always."

"Thank you, Cherrie." I said it with a smile, but I didn't know how to express how much her kindness always meant to me.

The menu was sitting on the table. I picked it up, looked it over, and realized someone was looking at me.

Cupid.

He was looking at me through the window. Our eyes were locked on each other. I glanced over at the empty side of the table and then back to him. He must have thought I was offering him a seat because one minute he was outside, the next he was sitting across from me, smiling.

"Thanks for the invite. I'm starving." Cupid's grin almost warmed my skin as I looked at him. But then I remembered his teasing.

I let out a sigh. "Just don't annoy me."

"No promises." He smirked at me and then waved at Cherrie as she walked up to the table. "Cherrie, I see you found her early this year."

"Why don't you let her rest before accosting her with your games?"

He wiggled his finger at her. "No can-do Mrs. Davis. I gotta make sure Daisy knows I care about her."

"Hello," I said. "I'm sitting right here. You can talk to me."

Cupid looked at me and nodded. "Apologies." His attention turned back to Cherrie. "Can I get one of your home-style burgers with fries?"

She nodded. "So, your usual, got it." She wrote something down and then smiled at me. "And you sweetie?"

"You know what? That sounds perfect. I'll have the same thing."

Cupid's lips curled into a large grin. "Damn, I love a woman who can eat."

"Okay, you have me trapped. I'm stuck here until I am done eating, so tell me. What is it you want from me this time?"

Cupid's eyes narrowed, and his smile turned into a sinister grin. "Daisy, I want to play a joke on the mayor. And I need your help to do it."

I put my hands out in front of my face and then pushed my head down face, palming myself. "Oh gods," I murmured into my hand.

"Now hear me out. I want you to host an egg hunt this year, except for the adults."

"Why?" I asked as I shook my head.

"Because people around here have been a little uptight lately. And I think the town could benefit from a little bit of sexual fun."

"Sexual fun?" I asked.

He nodded. "Yes."

"For shits and grins, if I said yes. What would this joke be?"

"I told you; you lay eggs for adults."

My face gave him a blank stare. "And you think I believe it would be a normal egg hunt?"

Cupid laughed. "True. Well, instead of candy in the eggs, it would be sex toys. We could have a town orgy."

"Are. You. Kidding. Me!?" I blurted out with a lot of emphasis on each word.

"Keep it down. But yes, that's what I want to do. Think about it. How much fun would it be?"

I didn't respond to him immediately. Cherrie had brought our food over to us and instead of responding, I opened my mouth and picked up my burger and took a bite from it.

Food, delicious food.

Cupid started talking more about this prank he wanted to

do. I listened, sort of. It wasn't a huge desire for me to piss off the demigod mayor, but Cupid had a point. Nothing ever changed in this town and the adults could use some fun.

"Fine, Cupid. I'm in. Just let me eat in peace."

"Yes! You're going to have so much fun. I promise."

I shook my head. "We'll see. Now please, let's just eat our food."

While we finished our food in silence, an idea struck me about mixing Cupid's plan with my own needs. I may not want to piss off the demigod, but a damsel in distress will do anything for attention. Our poor mayor did not know what was coming down the pike for him.

CHAPTER 2

MAYOR THOMPSON - LOCATION: HEMLOCK
VALLEY GAZEBO CENTER OF TOWN

"*R*ight there, that's right, hold it," I called out as my interns were hanging the Easter Egg Hunt signage up on the wooden beams. "We want to make sure everyone can see it from the street."

"Mayor Thompson, everyone will see it." The intern said in response.

"Straight! Keep it straight!" I barked out.

Once the sign was handled, I turned around and spotted the woman of the hour walking towards me.

"Daisy!" I exclaimed as I walked up to her, arms open wide. "Come here, my girl." I wrapped my arms around her tight and held her close. "Sally told me you had checked in this morning. I couldn't be more thrilled."

"It's good to see you too, Mayor."

"Are you planning anything fun for your monthly reprieve?" I stepped back and grinned down at her. She was always my favorite visitor. I had nothing to worry about. She came in, did her job, played a bit, and left. If all of my mythological creatures could be that easy, my life would be aces.

"Actually, yes, I have something planned."

My interest was piqued. "Oh, do tell!"

Daisy's face lit up. "I want to break the curse."

I couldn't stop the laugh that slipped out. I was too surprised. "I don't know if Andrew will be okay with that. You're one of his most valued prizes."

"I'm not a prize to be won. I'm a human."

I wiggled my finger at her. "My dear, you're a shifter at best. A bunny shifter. And you belong to him."

"But hear me out, I had an idea."

"Of course, as your mayor, I will listen to anything you want. But I am telling you, Mr. Jackson will not stand for anyone taking you from him."

Her lips curled into a grin, and she started batting her eyes. "Not even a god?"

I shook my head. "Don't get yourself any ideas there, missy. I will not interfere in property disputes such as this one."

"I'm not property. You damn well know I'm not. And I don't deserve to be tethered like this."

"From my point of view," I said, "you have it better than a lot. Look at genie's, stuck in a lamp. Or Jinn's who are trapped. Hell, even some leprechauns are only able to travel on a rainbow and never leave it. We can't all get our ways now, can we?"

"You can't think this is fair!" she cried out.

"Shhh, Daisy, stop. I can't have you crying like this. Everyone will think I made the water works start."

"But you did," she said, wiping her eyes. "I just want my freedom. I want to have a life of my own. You're a god why can't you help me?"

"Correction, I'm a demigod. I don't have endless powers."

"Your father does," she retorted.

"I'm not going to my old man to ask for a favor for someone else. I owe him too much as it is for my own items."

"Fine, but don't say I didn't warn you," Daisy huffed and crossed her arms.

"Warn me? Warn me about what? You didn't warn me at all. What's going on Daisy?"

She shook her head. "No, you won't help me. I won't help you. We aren't the friends, I thought."

I watched as she turned around and walked off.

"What was that all about?" Sally asked as she walked up to me.

"Honestly, I thought it was about her freedom, but now I don't know. Maybe she's having bunny hormones or something. Best I can tell, Daisy wants freedom, and she wants me to make it happen."

"You should. You should talk to Andrew."

I turned toward my secretary in shock. "You are serious? You who tell me to stay out of messes that don't need my political or governmental help want me to get involved in a domestic issue over property?"

Sally smiled. "I adore Daisy. And it's been over a hundred years. She deserves some freedom."

"She has freedom, once a year for a month."

"You know what I mean. William," she laid her hand on my arm, "think about it."

I watched my secretary walk off to tend to another item on our checklist for the Easter Egg Hunt weekend. I did not want to get involved in this matter at all. Not one bit. Hopefully Sally wouldn't push me.

DAISY - LOCATION: THE ATTIC

THERE WAS SOMETHING EERIE about being around so many vampires, but I needed to talk to Cupid, and I knew that this was his favorite place to cause trouble. Vampire sex clubs were dangerous for humans, but I wasn't a human, completely. Hopefully, no one would want to destroy the Easter Bunny.

"Well well well," I heard someone say from behind me in a teasing yet sinister tone.

I turned around to see one of the main vampires in charge of the town Onyx with his arms crossed, smirking at me.

"Good morning to you, too." I smiled and crossed my arms. "I'm looking for a man."

"Well, you came to the right place, bunny." He walked up to me in his standard intimidation form.

"Where's your better half?" I asked, trying to be polite.

"She's at work." He lowered his arms and then smiled at me. "Nice to see you, Daisy. Who are you looking for?"

"Cupid."

"If you need a hook up on your monthly vacation, just say the word. I got tons of guys who would want to taste you."

I shook my head. "No, I need Cupid. We have a previous discussion that needs finishing."

"Don't say I didn't offer to find you a better guy. But your boy is in the back in a semi-private booth enjoying the show. Be careful."

I smiled at Onyx. "Thank you. I'll find him."

Talking with vampires was something that took time getting used to. Lucky for me, I had time to spare. I spotted Cupid off in the distance and made a beeline straight to him.

"We need to talk," I said before sitting down.

"Here?" He looked at me sideways before turning his attention back to the women dancing on stage.

"Yes. This is important."

"If it's so important, then you should have my undivided attention. I can meet you in an hour. I got things to tend to right now."

I looked around. "What needs tending to?"

He laughed. "Me."

I rolled my eyes. "You're not even with someone."

"Yet. I will be. I'm just waiting for the right person." He cut his eyes towards me. "Unless you're the right person."

I felt my cheeks flush red as he looked at me with that gaze. "Cupid," I said, almost in a breathless tone. "Are you being serious?"

He adjusted himself, and his smirk grew even wider. "I'm dead serious. You want my full attention, and I want yours."

I licked my lips and knew that for this moment, it would be worth letting temptation win. "Fine."

He wiggled his finger at me in the come-hither fashion. I scooted out of the booth and watched as he adjusted his legs, opening them wide for me. Knowing what he wanted, I knelt and smiled. Cupid brought his fingers to my cheek and lightly stroked my skin.

"I've wanted this for many years," he confessed.

Cupid hadn't been sly about his desires. I knew he had wanted me. And the reality was, I knew Cupid wanted everyone. It was kind of in the design of what his mythological powers were all about. But I ignored all that to focus on the task at hand.

"I know," I responded before using my hands to release his cock from his pants. It was an impressive size, what sprung free from his jeans. Out of an instinct, I licked my lips and then lowered my head to work on the task at hand.

His scent was overpowering. As I moved my head up and down, I took in his musky scent through my nostrils. There was something about how it stirred my hormones in my body. I felt my body heat inside as I went further into this activity.

As my mouth oozed saliva on his cock, my hands worked mercilessly to jack him off while sucking his cock. I closed my eyes to focus on concentration and then I felt Cupid's hands fisting my hair. His fingers were wrapping my strands around them, and he was now controlling my speed.

Up and down, harder, faster, over and over. I was getting motion sickness from the ferocity of the force Cupid was controlling me. I could taste my reward moments away. His precum filled my mouth and my body craved it. I let one of my hands slip off of his cock and moved it between my legs. I started rubbing my pussy with my fingers, the jeans I was wearing causing friction. Needing more, I slipped my hand into my pants, parted my lips, and fingered my aching clitoris.

Within seconds, we both came together, releasing our mutual pleasure.

CHAPTER 3

CUPID - LOCATION: THE ATTIC

J loved how her mouth felt on my cock, sucking away until I erupted into her mouth. It had been years since I felt someone's mouth so powerful working my dick over. When I exploded into her warm hole and felt her throat contracting around my head, I could have died and gone to heaven. She had the suction of a professional, and I wanted even more.

"Fuck me," I moaned while my hand fingered her hair. Oh, how marvelous this was.

So much of my life was putting people together for romance. Receiving anything on my own wasn't something that happened to too often and feeling it now was splendid.

"Cupid," she murmured with a mouth full of cum and my dick still inside.

The vibrations from her larynx sent my hormones into overdrive. I wanted more.

"Shh, my sweet little rabbit. Let's enjoy this for a moment or two more before we speak."

I let my fingers caress her cheeks. Her eyes had droplets of tears at the edges from the perfect blowjob she had just performed.

When my dick fell out of her mouth and the moment of pure enjoyment passed, my heartbeat slowed down and my breathing returned to normal. Daisy moved her hands delicately as she pushed my now limp dick back into my pants for me. After I zipped them up, I signaled to the other side of the booth, asking her to join me.

"Thank you, Daisy. That was perfect."

She smiled at me. Maybe she had a little praise kink because her eyes lit up as I said it.

"Thank you. That was fun. I haven't had that kind of fun in quite some time."

It was my turn to grin. "Well, if you're looking for more of it in your short time with us this year, I'm all for it."

"Maybe," she smirked. "But I want to talk to you about what we discussed earlier. Playing the prank."

I nodded my head. "Yes, are you willing to do it?"

"Yes. And I want it to be so crazy that the mayor will make a deal with me."

"A deal to cut you free?"

She nodded her head. "Yes."

"And what's in it for me?"

"Well," she waved her hand at my dick, "I did just do that."

I laughed. "You did, but I could get head anytime I wanted."

"Cupid."

"Daisy," I said back to her.

I loved how worked up she seemed to get, and it was making this so much more fun. I loved when a woman could put up a good fight.

"Seriously, Cupid. You must help me. No one else could even come close to this level of help. We're friends. How many years now?"

I smiled at her. I was going to help her. It was not just the right thing to do but having a woman who wanted me for me and not because of my powers was something you couldn't put a price on.

"I'll do it. But there are conditions."

She nodded her head. "I assumed there would be." As Daisy thought, I gave her time to process everything. "What conditions?"

"When this is all over and you've earned your freedom." I stopped to think about how to word what I wanted properly. "When you're free, I want you to move in with me."

"From one master to another, then?" She said it in a tone that told me she didn't love this idea.

"I don't want to force you. I wouldn't be your master. But you must admit, we've always gotten along well enough and we're friends. Where else would you go?"

"I haven't gotten that far in my planning."

"Fine, how about this? You move in with me, but as a roommate and not a lover. Unless that's what you end up wanting." When she opened her mouth to speak, I raised my hand up and stopped her. "I don't want you for sex. I mean, well, I do. But not like this. I'm not asking for sex in return for freedom. I hate when we're trapped. So, I will help you for free. And in return, I will just hope you give us a chance."

Daisy's face was beautiful, and watching her think about my offer got me horny. I wasn't sure why. Maybe it was the setting we were in and everything that had just happened, but I needed to fuck her.

"Okay, deal."

I let my reaction lead the way with a smile plastered across my face. "Perfect."

"Don't get any ideas, but I really need to fuck you right now."

Of all the things I thought Daisy was going to say, that

wasn't on the list. "Oh," I purred out, "you do?" There was no hiding my excitement. I loved hearing it. And, of course, she needed to be fucked. She had been locked up for a fucking year.

"Don't make me beg."

I stood up from the booth, reached my hand out to her, and pulled her into a standing position. My arms moved around her waist, and I lowered my head, sealing our lips together in a kiss. She tasted like me, and I loved it.

"Why don't you come back to my house tonight? I could show you everything you would be in for. Well, not everything. Gotta leave you wanting more after all."

I could see it in her eyes. Daisy wanted to say yes. She wanted to come back with me. Her hesitation was obvious, but I didn't understand why.

"What's stopping you?"

"I don't know," she said.

Our fingers laced together. I brought her hand up to my mouth and placed a kiss on the back of it. "I'll only bite when you ask me to. Promise." I winked at her right there at the end.

The curvature of her lips forming a smile told me that sealed the deal.

"Alright, take me home."

"As you wish," I said before pulling her close and vanishing with her in my arms.

When we reappeared in my living room, I barely caught Daisy before passing out. I forgot that transporting like that for the first few times took a lot of out humans. I carried her in my arms to my bedroom, where I laid her down on the bed. Gingerly, I removed her shoes and socks and then pulled the covers down from under her and tucked her into bed.

The romping I so eagerly awaited would be postponed now until later. She would sleep for a few hours.

"Sleep sweet Daisy." I leaned over and placed a kiss on her lips. She looked perfect in my bed.

Turning the lights out and walking back into my living room, I sat down on my couch, pulled a movie up on the television and let the comedy of Chevy Chase tame down my horniness. There was plenty of time for action. No need to be disappointed.

CHAPTER 4

DAISY - LOCATION: HEMLOCK VALLEY GAZEBO

*J*t was the morning of Easter, and Cupid and I had the perfect plan. He had helped me with the magic needed to make all of my Easter eggs contain larger items. We also tweaked the spell to make sure if anyone under the age of eighteen picked up the egg, a large bunny shaped chocolate would appear. I wanted my freedom but not at the expense of causing any harm to the children.

Not that I would say I was aiming to harm any adult. Just make them insanely horny and possibly start an orgy riot in the center of town.

"Alright, the last egg of my batch is set out," Cupid said, walking up to me.

"Excellent. The mayor will have to take me seriously now."

"Mayor Thompson has taken no one seriously in years. Don't be upset if it doesn't work out. I told you, when we woke up today, he hates being bullied."

"As do I. And I hate being a slave to Mister Andrew Jackson, Postmaster." I crossed my arms, pushed my hip out, and grinned. "Everyone will have to take me seriously now."

"I need to warn you," Cupid said.

"Warn me?" I asked. "About what?" I felt a wave of concern wash over me.

"You know I love the concept of love, right?"

Nodding my head. "It's kind of your whole schtick."

Cupid smiled. "Glad you see it that way. I added one other caveat on the spell. There will be no cheating in this orgy of yours. If someone is in a committed relationship of any kind, they are only getting freaky in public with their partner."

It was annoying and adorable how much he stuck to his values. But I couldn't argue with him. I needed him for this plan to work, so I had no choice but to accept this new condition. "That's fine. I should have thought about it myself. I want to be able to live in this town when this is all done, after all. Don't need the townies coming at me with a pitchfork."

"Great. Now that this little matter is settled, you want to come sit over there with me and watch the mayhem begin?" He pointed to the park bench on W. Jasmine Dr. in front of the sherif's office.

"You want to sit in front of the cops?"

Cupid laughed. "What better way to see all the action unfold than at the local dispatch office?"

"What about if we go there instead?" pointing to the bench on N. Lily St in front of the Hemlock Inn.

"Fine, but don't say I didn't warn you. The best seat in the house was by the coppers."

I laughed. "If I am mistaken, I will gladly say you were right."

"You better get used to that," Cupid smirked at me.

"Used to what?"

He put his arm around me, pulled me close and planted

a kiss on my lips that was powerful enough to knock a typical human's socks off. "Telling me I am right. When you're free, and we can be together, I'm going to be right a lot."

I wasn't sure if it was his magical powers that blew me away or if it was the intimacy and romance of the situation, but there I was, being whisked away into a gooey puddle by Mister Love Maker himself. My whole body tingled just from that one kiss. I would be a fool to turn him down, so I didn't. My arms found their way around his neck. I pressed my breasts into his chest and kissed him back with all the effort I could muster.

"Maybe I need to go pick up one of those eggs and see what treat is in store for us?" Cupid said as he was kissing my chin and then down my jawline to my earlobe. "We could get this party started right here."

"Cupid," I moaned in response to his mouth sucking on my earlobe. The truth was, I didn't need any toys to get riled up. He had my juices flowing already, and all we had done is kiss.

"Yes Daisy? I love it when you moan my name." He took my arm from around his neck and brought my hand down to his crotch. "You feel what you do to me? You've always done this to me."

He was harder than I could picture. Maybe it was the pants adding girth or something. But it was intimidating and calling my name all at once.

"Yes," I panted.

Cupid looked around and saw that no one was around us. He pushed us quickly across the grass to the gazebo in the middle of the park. His hands were all over my body, squeezing me. "I'm changing your pants into a skirt."

"What?" But before I could ask anything else, I felt the cool air touching my legs. I was magically changed from pants to a skirt, and I noticed he dispensed my panties without even asking me. Laughing, I said, "Did you forget something?"

He shook his head no grinning. "I don't forget any detail. You'll get your real clothes back soon. After I'm done with you."

My stomach was now pressed against the half wall of the gazebo. I was looking out into one section of the park. As expected, I felt the skirt fly up in the air and land on my back. My bare ass was now exposed to the cool air, and Cupid's hand came down unexpectedly, spanking my cheek, hard.

"Owe!" I yelped.

"That's for being difficult all these years."

He spanked me again, causing me to cry out once more.

"What was that one for?"

Cupid's laughter made my skin pebble in goosebumps. "I enjoyed watching your ass giggle."

And then I felt it, his hard cock thrusting inside of me. I hadn't even comprehended what we were doing, and his large, hard cock was pushing in and out of my pussy. My soaking pussy.

"My goodness, you're like a faucet! Just full of water."

Cupid was a vigorous man, and each time he rammed his cock inside of me, it was like bells going off in my body. He made every inch of me tingle in delight and, before much time passed; I was creaming his cock with a delicious reward.

"Fuck, yes!" He cried out.

His hands held onto my hips and wouldn't let me go. We were inseparable, no space between our two bodies as he unloaded his cum inside of me. It was a glorious reward for such a great moment.

"Ahem," we heard someone from behind us.

I didn't want to turn and look. I knew the voice, and I knew what was coming next. Cupid didn't seem to care. He caressed my ass cheek while the voice of my slave owner, Andrew Jackson, started talking.

"Daisy, what on earth are you doing? This reflects badly on me. Seriously, can you not just act like I taught you decorum?"

"You're dismissed," Cupid said to Andrew as his cock slid out of my pussy and pants reappeared on my legs. "She doesn't need your services anymore. She has a new master. Isn't that right, my sweet bunny?"

I turned around in Cupid's arms and let him kiss me. I didn't say anything, just kissed this man back with all the same force he gave me.

"Well, we will see about this bad behavior when you're back in your cage." Andrew stormed off in a huff of literal smoke.

"Goading him probably wasn't smart," I said.

Cupid shrugged. "As you can see, I'm not scared of him. This plan will work, and we will be together."

"I really hope so." There was a smirk on Cupid's face as I noticed he was now watching the towns people behind me.

Turning around, I saw several families out hunting for the eggs. Off to one side, I noticed two adults standing around talking. A golden egg magically appeared at the man's foot. I knew Cupid made that happen. We watched as the woman leaned over and picked up the egg.

"She's gonna love the bullet inside that egg." Cupid's voice was full of pride at our prank.

Sure enough, when she opened the egg and a silver bullet fell into her hand, her face lit up. We watched as the two of them started going at it right there on the grass. Off to our left, another couple had opened an egg and were getting frisky.

Before I knew what was happening, there were ten couples having sex on the lawn of the town.

"DAISY!"

We heard the mayor's voice booming out over the town. He appeared magically beside us. I supposed as a demigod he could do that sort of thing.

"What in the actual fuck are you doing with this year's Easter hunt?"

"I want my freedom." I shrugged my shoulders and then turned back to the show in front of us.

"Daisy, I warn you!"

"You warn her about what?" Cupid asked. "She asked for your help. You didn't help her, now she is having some fun. Sounds to me like there is an easy solution to all of this."

"I don't interfere in those matters; Daisy, you know this."

More people were now out on the grass all over the center of town. Things were getting pretty graphic and luckily the parents of the kids that were out had quickly ushered the young ones away.

"Free me." I didn't feel like anything else needed said. He knew what I wanted, and he could see the result of me not getting it.

"I don't like being blackmailed. You're using trickery and I don't approve."

Cupid laughed. "This from the demigod who uses his powers whenever it suits him?"

There was a lot of strength feeling the comfort of Cupid defending me. That hadn't happened since my boyfriend was killed so many years ago.

"Fine. FINE! I will free you, but stop all of this now."

I shook my head. "Free me, then I'll stop it. And make it so no one can ever enslave me in any other way again."

Cupid turned me around and kissed me. "Oh, I'm going to enslave you as my dirty, bad girl once this is all done."

I laughed. "Good."

Mayor Thompson looked angrier than I had ever seen another being, but he said nothing. He just waved his hands, and I felt the freedom wash over me. I hadn't felt this in so many hundreds of years that the sensation was overwhelming. Tears formed in my eyes, and I cried. I couldn't hold my weight and as I started to collapse, Cupid picked me up in his arms.

"I got this."

Suddenly, everyone stopped having sex on the grass. The folks of the town were all dressed and standing, holding normal Easter eggs.

"None of them will remember anything," Cupid said to Mayor Thompson.

"Good. Now, go before I change my mind. I won't forget what you two did to me here today."

"Neither will I." My voice was shaky as the tears rushed down my cheeks. I was finally free.

"NO! DAISY!" We heard Andrew Jackson screaming as he ran across the grass. "Get back here!"

"Take me away," I said to Cupid.

"With pleasure." Cupid had us appear in his bedroom, and as he sat me down on the bed, I felt a sense of peace.

I was home.

"What do you want to do with your first moments of freedom?"

There was only one right answer. "You."

He grinned at me and snapped his fingers. We were both naked, and he was hard again, ready to go.

"God, that's an amazing skill you have." I said, looking down grinning at his erection.

"Hey, he loves love. What can I say?"

As Cupid pushed me onto the mattress and slipped his hard dick back into my moist pussy, I realized this was how my life was going to be from now on. And I was perfectly okay with that.

The End.

ABOUT SUNNY

Sunny A. Morgan is a best-selling author and furbaby mama, who has been profession-ally writing for over a decade. She recently took the leap from her business career and returned to her West Virginia mountains to write full-time. Known for her age-gap, dominate/submis-sive erotic tales, she loves weaving sexy tales for her readers.

You can find her on most social media platforms and through my Linktree

ABOUT SKYLAR

As a spicy romance author, Skylar Quinn has learned the art of detail. It's the details that matter most in a story. It's those 'details' that determine the heat level. And Skylar isn't afraid to bring the flames to her works of art. She is an Apple & Amazon best-selling author for several of her short story series. It's in the world of spice that Skylar has found her calling. Deep down, though, she will always be a paranormal girl at heart. With a new story released every Friday, Skylar strives to give her readers what they're looking for. Spice, and lots of it.

Purchase Skylar's books here: https://payhip.com/Crush Pub/collection/skylar-quinn-s-books

Substack: SkylarQ.Substack.com

Skylar's website: linktr.ee/skylar_quinn

Skylar's email: quinnskylar23@gmail.com

She enjoys hearing from her readers and will always take plot suggestions from fans!

KINDLE UNLIMITED STORIES BY SUNNY A MORGAN

The Library

Follow these three couples as they explore their fantasies and instant lust turns into instant love.

Read the series on Amazon The Library Series Link

Hemlock Valley (With Skylar Quinn)

A small town Paranormal Erotica series with twists and turns that make you forget what real small town life is all about.

Merry Kinkmas (With Skylar Quinn)

Santa isn't the only one who gets off this year! Six sexy stories that celebrate all the fun ways Santa can 'enjoy' himself this holiday season..

KINDLE UNLIMITED STORIES BY SKYLAR QUINN

Untying The Knot One Couple's BDSM Journey (With Logan Black)

Erik and Allie have two decades together and through the love of books, start exploring the joys of BDSM and erotica as they spice up their sex life, while maintaining their family routine.

Hemlock Valley (With Sunny A Morgan)

A small town Paranormal Erotica series with twists and turns that make you forget what real small town life is all about.

Temptation Tuesday

From backyards, to cruise ships, construction sites, the confessional, and all places in-between, Temptation Tuesday is a series celebrating erotica and all the pleasure it brings

The Interns

Summertime is when the college coeds snag internships. With this marketing firm, the interns get one on one instruction in all the ways pleasing a boss pays off…

The Cuckquean

Women can have fun too! This series celebrates those women who just want to see their husbands shared with all their friends.

Merry Kinkmas (With Sunny A Morgan)

Santa isn't the only one who gets off this year! Six sexy stories that celebrate all the fun ways Santa can 'enjoy' himself this holiday season..

Stand Alone Stories

An Orc for Halloween

When my best friend asked me to help her decorate for a Halloween party, I didn't expect to hear a secret that would change everything and leave me looking for someone else to spend the evening with.

That's when he walked in. There was something about this man. Maybe it was his massive size that made his orc costume look so real. Or maybe it was the potent attraction unlike anything I'd ever felt before.

I should have known something was different about my best friend's guests, but betrayal blinded me until the monster had me in his arms.

And I wasn't sure I ever wanted to leave... no matter what my friend did to try to stop us.

CRUSHED: Skylar Quinn

Ranch and Logan aren't in Kansas anymore...

Except, sike! They totally are. It's been a long road trip from Houston to Wamego, Kansas, but when the Crush Queen Skylar Quinn requests an Oz-themed crushing, who are they to refuse?

Their ultimate destination at the end of this Yellow Brick Road? The Wizard of Oz Museum, of course. And these wanton friends mean help their gorgeous Dorothy "get off" to see the wizard in more ways than one.

But wait—shouldn't a naughty Dorothy have three lustful companions? Leave it to Logan to find a "tin man" to round out their fantastic foursome.

See how Skylar Quinn gets initiated into the Lollipop Guild plus much, much more in CRUSHED - Skylar Quinn.

ALSO BY SUNNY A MORGAN

SERIES:

My Husband's Best Friend Series Link

Not My Series Link

Naughty Bosses Series Link

Sanctuary Security Series Link

The Library BDSM Club Series Link

Merry Kinkmas Series

Hemlock Valley Series Link

Hotwife/Cuckold/Freeuse Series

Getting Dirty With My Professor

STANDALONE BOOKS:

Submitting To My Stalker

My Older Neighbor: Age Gap

Tempting Him Bundle

Snow For Christmas

Ganging Cyn

Claiming The Nanny

The Auction

Tempted & Taken

Tempting Him

Claiming Sunny

My Nephew's Bride

My Ex-Boyfriend's Dad

My Ex-Wife's Daughter

Tempting The Man Of The House

Keep Me

ALSO BY SKYLAR QUINN

≈

Hotwife Book 9 (Hall Pass)

Hotwife Book 10 (Bowling & Buddy's)

Hotwife Book 11 (My Wife Explores Some Fun)

Hotwife Book 12 (Caught At The Bar)

≈

First Sight

Hotwife

Cuckold

Wife Swap

≈

Holiday Series

Cheating Husbands: Taking My Neighbor's Daughter on Thanksgiving

Hotwife & Cheating Husbands

Hubby Cheated on Thanksgiving

More The Merrier on Thanksgiving

Taking the Babysitter for Christmas

≈

Written with Sean Geist

Wicked Lessons

Hotwife Pool Party

Business Affair

Extramarital Fun (Print Collection of WL, HWPP, BA)

Most Dangerous Game

Most Dangerous Affair

≈